The Obsessed Alphas Collection

Books 5-8

Claiming Callie

Taken by the CEO

Forbidden Passion

The Guardian's Temptation

Lacy Jane Publishing

Contents

Claiming Callie

Lacy Jane

Lacy Jane Publishing

Contents

Callie

♥

"**Y**ou are mine!" *Rex yells as he thrusts fully inside me. I feel myself gush with pleasure as he slams deeper and deeper. The tension builds, making my pussy throb harder and harder. I know I'm building up to a huge orgasm; unlike any I've ever experienced before. He finally screams my name, filling me up with his seed and making me come hard, gushing my juices all over him. I nearly black out from the pleasure.*

"I love you, baby," he says, kissing me deeply. "Never gonna let you go. I already need to fuck you again."

"Yes!" I scream as he thrusts his huge cock inside me once more. He's finally mine. We are finally together. He's everything I've ever wanted. I smile up at him as he takes me again and again...

My alarm blares, waking me from a great dream. It felt so real. I realize that I actually orgasmed in my sleep, and the bed is really wet. I just wish it was from both of us, like I had just dreamt.

You see, I'm in love with Rex Cameron. Yes, that Rex Cameron. Former tight end for the Dallas Cowboys; known to me as Uncle Rex. He isn't actually related to me, but has been my dad's best friend since high school, so he is my honorary uncle. He's like family, and has known me my whole life. And therein lies the problem.

Rex has been a big part of my life since I was born. Unfortunately, he has lived in Dallas for the last fifteen years, so I don't get to see him as often as I'd like. Last year, though, he finally retired from football and started his own construction company back here in Langsford, Florida. He has been gone a lot lately to tie up some loose ends in Texas, but this weekend, he is finally coming back for good.

He will be staying with us for a bit while he looks for a house. I haven't seen him in person for several months, and I miss him terribly. I'm looking forward to spending a lot of time with him.

Rex is larger than life, and the nicest guy on the planet. He even has a children's charity. He spends a lot of time visiting sick kids in the hospital. It's enough to make a girl's ovaries explode. He is kind, selfless, fun, and handsome; so fucking handsome.

At six foot eight with a massive frame, you would think he would have been way too slow for the NFL. Instead, he was the fastest runner in the league. He is always ranked in the top ten tight ends of all time, and often the top ten players of all time.

They say he had the best hands in the NFL. Believe me, he has made some unbelievable catches. Whenever they talk about how talented his hands are, though, all I can think about is having them all over my naked body.

I have always loved Uncle Rex, but over the last few years, it has morphed into a different kind of love. There is nothing remotely familial about the lust I feel coursing through my veins whenever he's near. Even watching him play football each week on tv was enough to inspire my fantasies for months on end. I have gotten myself off countless times to visions of him. He's better than any porn out there.

I have a whole collection of pictures of him stored on my phone. I use them anytime I need inspiration. My favorites are any of the pictures showing him bare chested. That muscular chest and his huge arms? Oh. My. God. I can't even express how sexy he looks. And don't even get me started on the Calvin Klein ad he did in just his underwear. All I have to do is look at that picture, which really shows off the monster between his legs, and I'm on the verge of orgasm. He's my obsession.

I know, I know. It's unrealistic. He's rich, handsome, and famous. He could have anyone he wants. Why on earth would he want me? I'm just a girl he's known forever that sells jewelry on Etsy and still lives at home with her dad. He probably has famous actresses and models hitting on him on a daily basis. I should probably just forget about him and find someone else.

The problem is he is so damn handsome and wonderful, no other man can possibly compare. I know that none of the boys I went to school with even came close. That's why, at the ripe old age of twenty-two, I am still a virgin. I am saving myself for Uncle Rex. I know it's crazy, but he's the only man I have ever wanted, and ever will.

As much as I want him, though, I'm afraid he'll only ever see me as the little girl with pigtails he used to push on the swings. I will most likely embarrass myself, but I am determined to finally get Rex to see me as a woman; not a little girl. He's everything I've ever wanted. I have to try; even if I end up getting my heart demolished in the end.

Rex

I turn into John and Callie's driveway. I am looking forward to seeing them. My parents died in a car crash when I was only five. Sadly, I only have very vague memories of them. Since I had no living relatives, I bounced from foster home to foster home until my freshman year of high school, when I met John.

For some unknown reason, we hit it off right away. Maybe it was because we both loved football, or because we were great at building things in shop class. After a while, he brought me home to meet his folks. They ended up becoming my foster family, so I spent the majority of high school with John and his parents.

Jim and Elsie Stevens were kind, caring people. They had John later in life, and their world revolved around him and me. Jim was the one who encouraged me to pursue football, and Elsie taught me how loving a mother could be. They've been gone for several years now, but I still miss them both terribly.

John and Callie Stevens are the only two people left in the world that I consider family. Sure, I've made some good friends in football, and have guys over to watch sports on occasion, but nobody compares to them.

I get out of the car and hear a high pitched squeal. I see a blur of silky blonde hair as Callie flies at me, wrapping her arms and legs around me like a monkey. "Hey, squirt," I laugh, hugging her tightly to me. She steps back and smiles brightly up at me. She's a foot or so shorter than me, so I have to lean down to her level.

"I've missed you," she whispers, pressing a quick kiss against my lips. It's innocent enough, but between the kiss and catching a whiff of her vanilla shampoo, my cock immediately hardens. *Shit!* I keep enough space between us so she won't discover that just being near her immediately turns my cock to stone.

Here's the deal. I've known Callie her entire life; literally. I was there in the hospital when Sandy gave birth to her. I have always loved her like a niece. That is, until the last couple of years.

I don't know what the hell happened. All I know is that one minute, she was a kid, and the next, she was a smoking hot siren that I desperately wanted. When I saw her at her twentieth birthday party, I no longer felt anything remotely paternal toward her. What I felt was the overwhelming lust a man feels toward a woman he wants to fuck. Badly.

She has a stunning hourglass figure. I hadn't realized it until that night when I saw that sexy little body in a sundress that was practically painted on. The dress had a cherry pattern all over it; fucking cherries, for God's sake! All I could think about was sex. Sex and Callie.

I felt like a pervert having those thoughts about her. She's practically family, after all. That's why I have done my best to stay away from her for the last couple of years, even though I had hoped and prayed that it was a one time problem. I'm finding out quickly, though, that the pull I felt toward her then hasn't gone away. If anything, it has intensified.

Her beautiful smile lights up her face. Her blonde hair touches her shoulders, and her sapphire eyes sparkle with happiness. She is definitely not a kid anymore. Her womanly figure has my body on high alert. Her huge breasts and voluptuous hips should look too big for her small frame, but they don't. She looks fucking perfect, and perfect for fucking.

Jesus. I make a vow to myself that I will do everything I can to keep my desire in check and my dick in my pants. The last thing I want to do is lose the most important woman in my life because I'm lusting after her.

I have stayed away for the better part of two years, but I have kept tabs on her. I stalk her on social media. She doesn't post much, but I save each and every picture she posts and look at them over and over again. I jack myself off nightly to pictures of her.

I was hoping that I would be disappointed when I saw her in the flesh again; that she wouldn't be as stunning as I remembered. Yep. She's not. She's even better. She's everything I have ever wanted. She is my fucking obsession.

Callie

♥

I am so glad that Rex is here, even if I haven't gotten to spend much time with him yet. He got here yesterday, and just the feel of his arms around me was enough to set my body on fire.

I try to concentrate on my jewelry rather than Rex, while Taylor Swift blares from my bluetooth speaker. I bebop along, while putting everything together. I have several orders to fill, so I'm trying to get caught up.

"What are you doing, squirt?" I jump. Damn, I hate when he calls me that!

"Jeez. You scared me, Uncle Rex. Just working."

"Can I see?"

I smile. "Sure." I show him the different necklaces I have created; each in various stages of completion. I get excited sharing my work with anyone; but especially him. I shouldn't care what other people think about my jewelry, but his opinion means a lot to me.

"Callie, these are gorgeous. I had no idea you were so talented."

His praise makes me feel warm and fuzzy inside. "Thank you. It started out as a side hustle, but when I couldn't keep up with the orders anymore, I left college to pursue it full time. I love it."

"That's great, baby. I'm so proud of you." He hugs me to him, stroking my hair and making me tingle all over. I reach up and run my hand along his dark, well-trimmed beard. I can't help myself. It's just as soft as I thought it would be. I stroke his cheek before dragging my nails across his scalp. I feel a shiver go through him. His lips are so close. He looks at me with a serious expression. "Callie, sweetheart, what are you doing?"

"Just touching you, Uncle Rex. Is that okay?" I ask, batting my eyelashes at him; the very picture of innocence.

He takes a deep breath. "It's more than okay, baby. That's the fucking problem."

"What do you mean?" I ask, licking my lips.

"This is what I mean," he says, pulling me against him and taking my mouth hungrily with his. My entire body feels like it's on fire. He strokes his hands up and down my sides, making my center throb with need. It's even better that I have imagined and, believe me, I've imagined this *a lot*.

He holds me against him, rubbing his hard cock against my pussy. He's huge and hard, and feels oh, so good. My panties are drenched in seconds. We kiss for a few minutes before we hear Dad calling for him. "Rex, where did you go?"

He pulls away quickly. "Shit, Callie. I'm so sorry. I shouldn't have done that. This should never have happened." He backs out of the garage, clearly trying to escape from me as soon as possible. I hear the front door slam as he goes back inside the house.

I touch my tingling lips and try to catch my breath from his sensual onslaught. "Oh, Uncle Rex. This definitely should have happened, and if I have anything to say about it, it will happen again and again," I vow quietly to myself.

Rex

I shouldn't have kissed Callie. I definitely shouldn't have dry humped her like a dog in heat. *Crap.* I need to get my head on straight and go back to seeing her as a kid, not a woman. Easier said than done. I know that as soon as she walks toward me and John the next day, ready to go sailing with us.

Her gorgeous breasts bounce enticingly in her sundress, causing my cock to stiffen. Again. *Shit!* I can't seem to be around her without my cock being at full mast. This is going to be tougher than I thought. She's the most beautiful thing I've ever seen. I just need to think of her as the kid I've known all my life; not the knockout I see in front of me.

The three of us spend the day together. John regales Callie with stories about us in our youth, making her laugh hysterically. I love the sound of her laughter. I want to hear it every day. We have a lot of fun together. These are my two favorite people in the world, after all. I love being with them. I just have to get this obsession with Callie under control.

I do a pretty good job ignoring my urges until we get off the boat. John is still on board as I help her down. She ends up sliding against my body, all the way down. Her breath catches when she feels my hard cock rub against her core. "Oh, Uncle Rex. You feel so good," she whispers into my ear, rubbing against me.

I look for John and see that he is still below deck. I pull Callie behind the storage shed, where we are hidden from view, and kiss her with desperation. My mouth takes hers again and again. I pick her up and hold her sweet ass in my hands as I thrust against her warm little pussy.

"Fuck, baby," I say against her mouth. "You are all I can fucking think about. I just want to strip you and fuck your sweet little pussy. I want inside you so bad." I know it's wrong, but right now, I don't give a shit.

"Oh, Uncle Rex," she moans. "Me, too. I want you so much." She rubs her pussy against me, seeking release. I thrust hard against her until I pinch her clit, making her spiral. She cries out, making me come like a teenager. After a few moments, we hear John calling.

We break apart, sucking in deep breaths. I set her down, kissing the top of her head, and giving her a quick hug. "Let's go, sweetheart." We catch up with John. As we help him carry supplies back to the car, I do my best not to let myself look at her for too long. It's not going to take John long to figure out that I'm lusting after his daughter if I keep looking at her like I plan on devouring her.

This is getting out of hand. I can't keep my hands to myself. My dick is still hard as a rock. I think of everything I can to soften it up-baseball stats, Star Trek, black-eyed peas. As soon as I look over at her, though, I'm back in the same state. I have a big fucking problem. I want Callie desperately, and I don't see that going away anytime soon.

Callie

♥

I had so much fun yesterday with Rex. I was so happy when he kissed me again, and shocked when he dry humped me until I came. I am so happy that he wants me, too. I want him to be my first, last, and only lover. In order for that to happen, I need more time alone with him, and I need to turn up the heat; like, now.

With my incredibly pale skin, I'm not much of a sunbather. I need to get Rex's attention, though, so I'm pulling out all the stops. I mean, what's the use in having a pool if you can't use it to seduce the man of your dreams? I walk out to our pool in the sexiest swimsuit I own. It's white, skimpy, and nearly translucent. I've never even worn it before because it's *way* too over the top. For Rex, though, I will make an exception.

I have to say, the bra top pushes up my large breasts enticingly and the bikini bottoms make my ass look spectacular. I feel really sexy in this. Let's hope that he thinks so, too.

Rex walks outside and spots me. *Lord have mercy.* The man is in swim trunks with a towel wrapped around his waist. His seriously jacked arms and washboard abs are exposed. The butterflies in my stomach do a happy dance, and I feel moisture pool between my legs.

He mutters something under his breath about torture before coming out to join me. "Are you trying to kill me, baby doll?" he asks quietly, stroking a finger up my arm.

Dad pokes his head outside. "Hey, guys, I'm off to meet a date for lunch."

"Have fun!" I tell him. He deserves it. Mom died of cancer when I was only four. To the best of my knowledge, he hasn't had a relationship since. He loved my mom dearly and was beyond devastated when she passed away. After that, he put all his effort into raising me. I'm glad he's finally taking some time for himself.

Rex looks over at me. "Who does John have a date with?"

"No idea. He joined a dating site a few weeks ago, and has had several dates. Apparently, he's a hot property," I laugh.

"Good for him."

"I think so. I mean, someday I'll move out. I hate for him to be here all by himself."

"Yeah. It's not much fun being alone," he smiles at me. Oh, yeah. Time to put my plan into effect.

"Uncle Rex, do you think you can put some sunblock on me? I'm afraid I'll get burned," I say, looking up at him with my best innocent, puppy dog eyes.

"Sure thing, squirt. I didn't know that you even liked to sunbathe." Okay. He is back to calling me squirt. That's his way of pretending I'm still a kid. That is just not gonna work for me. Time to remind him that I am a woman; his woman.

"Well, I could use a little color, and they say vitamin d is good for you." He starts smoothing the cream over my shoulders. "Oh, my god. That feels so good," I moan. It takes everything I have not to thrust against the lounge chair to relieve the ache he is causing between my legs. Between the way he looks, his delicious scent, and the feel of his hands on my bare skin, I am seconds away from orgasming.

He pulls his hands away quickly. I look back at him beseechingly. "Please don't stop. You don't want me to look like a lobster, do you?" He resumes massaging the cream into my skin. The throbbing between my legs intensifies. I can hear his deep breaths and smell his sexy cologne.

"Can you put it on my front, too?" I ask, flipping onto my back and batting my eyelashes innocently at him.

I see him swallow hard. "Callie, I don't think that's such a good idea."

"But, Uncle Rex. I can't reach everywhere as easily as you can."

He starts rubbing my legs, then my stomach with the cream. I can feel my bikini bottoms dampening further with desire. The man of my dreams is rubbing my body with his magical hands. I moan loudly, and he jumps back like he's been burnt.

"What's wrong?"

"Nothing," he says, backing away from me. His towel drops. I look down and feel my sex clench with need. Rex's giant cock is tenting his swim trunks. Oh, lord. He's so huge and hard. I've never wanted anything like I want him right now.

"Uncle Rex," I say huskily, walking toward him. "You seem to have a problem. I want to help you with it." I kiss his mouth hungrily. He pulls me against him, taking my mouth over and over. He pushes me away after a few minutes, leaving us both gasping for air.

"Sweetheart, you don't know what you are saying," he says hoarse-ly.

Smiling up at him and licking my lips, I push his trunks down and take his engorged cock in my hands. Wow. It is fucking huge. I can feel it throbbing. My pussy is dripping with anticipation. The tip has precum leaking from it. I lean down and lick it, causing him to moan loudly.

"Sweetheart, we shouldn't," he starts to protest. I start again, licking it like the most delicious lollipop I've ever had, before sucking it down to the back of my throat. "Fuck!" he yells. He grabs my head and starts fucking my throat hard. My eyes are tearing up, but I don't care. I love it. I want to be his fuck toy. He can use me however he wants.

I gently roll his heavy balls in my hands. I feel his cock swelling up in my mouth and know that he's about to explode. Suddenly, we hear a car door close. "Oh, shit, baby. John is home. We need to stop." he says, trying to tug me off.

Instead of stopping, I double down on my efforts, sucking him off with everything I have until he groans and gushes stream after stream of cum into my mouth. I try to suck all of his creamy deliciousness down, but some of it drops onto my stomach and legs. I rub it in, moaning as I go. I tuck his cock back inside his swim trunks and lie back down on my lounge chair, smiling up at him.

Rex stands there looking stunned for several beats. When he hears my dad walking through the house, he snaps out of it and jumps into the cold water. No doubt, he is concerned about Dad seeing his huge erection. Even with all the cum he shot into my mouth, he's still gigantic and noticeably hard.

"Hey, guys. I forgot my wallet. I'll be back in a few hours."

A few minutes later, I hear his car pulling away. "Uncle Rex?" I ask, watching him stare back at me. Our heavy breaths seem loud in the silence.

"Callie, that cannot happen again. What the fuck was I thinking? I shouldn't have let you do that. It was so fucking wrong."

"Why was it wrong, Uncle Rex? We are both consenting adults. I loved it when you fucked my mouth. It made me so wet," I say, caressing my breasts as I watch him.

He groans as if he's in pain. "Fuck! Baby doll, you have to quit saying shit like that to me. It's not right. I'm twice your age and I'm practically related to you. Your dad would probably kill me, and I wouldn't blame him one bit."

"We are *not* related, and Dad isn't here right now. It's just you and me. I understand if we need to be discreet. I'm good at keeping secrets. Do you want to know a secret of mine?" He swallows and nods. "Sucking your big cock made me so horny. My pussy is dripping wet for you. See?" I push my fingers inside, and show him the glistening juices.

"Fuck, baby, you're not playing fair."

"All's fair in love and war," I smile. "Don't you want to taste me?" I look at him, lowering my lashes, moving my bottoms aside, and spreading my legs wide.

"Fuck!!! How am I supposed to resist you, baby? You are so fucking sexy! Look at that sweet little pussy of yours. It is soaking wet for me. I know I'm going to hell for this, but I have to taste you; just this once."

I nod emphatically. "Yes. Just this once. Whatever you say Uncle Rex. Yesss." I hiss as his mouth devours my pussy.

"**H**oly shit, baby doll. Your cunt is so fucking delicious," I say between licks. I devour her sweet honey hole with my mouth and tongue. It's the most delicious thing I've ever tasted. I could eat her every day for the rest of my life and never get tired of her sweet nectar. "You taste even better than I imagined."

I watch her beautiful face as she moans. She licks her lips and pushes me closer to her heat. I thrust a finger in. Her pussy sucks it in harder. She is so tight, it can barely fit. I push another in, fully fucking her with my fingers and tongue. "Come for me, baby." She screams, gushing her juices down my chin. I lick it all up, not wanting to miss a drop.

How can something so wrong feel so fucking right? I have never wanted a woman like I want Callie. I don't think I can hold off any longer. I'm claiming her as mine; right here, right now. I start to lower my trunks when the sound of a car door shatters the mood.

We both freeze for a moment. I quickly pull my trunks back up and put Callie's bikini bottoms back in place. "Thank you, Uncle Rex," she says, licking her lips. *Fuck!* I jump back into the pool to cool myself off.

John soon comes outside. "Hey, guys. She canceled on me. Can you believe it?"

He rattles on about what happened, but I'm not really listening. Callie stares at me like she wants to eat me up. How are we going to keep John from noticing what's happening between us? What was I thinking? What the hell have I done? And when can I do it again?

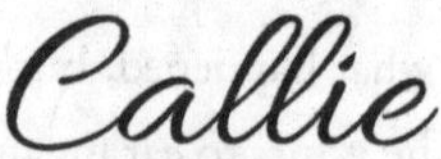

Callie

I can't believe I had Uncle Rex's big cock in my mouth, and I can't believe he ate my pussy. I've never given or received oral sex before. Let me tell you, both ways were incredible! If Dad hadn't come home early, Rex would have fucked me, right there on the lounge chair where anyone could have seen us. He was that desperate for me.

I'm afraid that now, since he's had time to think about it, he will revert back to trying to be a boy scout with me instead of the ravenous lover he was earlier. I have to do my best to keep that from happening.

The three of us sit at the kitchen table, eating the delicious pepperoni pizza we ordered from Jake's, the best pizzeria in town. I'm so nervous. Rex is, too. Thankfully, Dad talks enough for the three of us. Rex and I spend our time trying not to look like anything is different between us.

We all sit down to watch a movie. Before long, Dad falls asleep in his chair, like always. I'm already sitting next to Rex on the couch. I put a blanket over us and start touching his chest and stroking his cock. *Damn.* It's already hard and pulsing again. I need it inside me so badly. "Please, Rex. I need you," I whisper in his ear.

"Callie, you have to stop," he whispers through his moans. "We can't do this anymore, baby. It's wrong. I'm so sorry." With that, he gets up and goes to his room, closing and locking the door. *Shit! What do I do now?*

Rex

I spend the next three days making sure not to be alone with Callie. I've always had a lot of willpower, but it apparently doesn't apply to her. Callie Stevens is my kryptonite.

I've spent a lot of time over the last few days jacking myself off to thoughts of her. The memory of her hot little mouth sucking me off will still be fueling my fantasies when I'm in the nursing home someday.

That sweet little pussy. It tasted so good. I could live inside it. I want to claim her. I want to fuck her until she can feel me for weeks afterward. I want her to know that she belongs to me and me alone. I'm a sick, sick man.

She worships me, like a father figure. She is just confusing that with desire. She can't possible want a forty- year-old who runs a construction company. I know that she'll find someone her own age someday. Why does the thought of that make me nauseous?

I already know the answer. I can't stand the thought of her being with anyone else. Ever. I want her for myself; in every possible way. To be my lover, my wife, and the mother of my children. *Holy shit!* I don't know why I didn't see it before. I'm in love with her. What the fuck am I gonna do?

Callie

♥

Rex has been staying away from me for the last few days. It's very discouraging. Just when I was making progress, I'm back to square one. Actually, I'm back to minus ten or so, considering he doesn't even want to be in the same room with me.

"Goodnight, Dad," I say, kissing him on the cheek. I leave the kitchen and run into my dream man in the flesh. "Goodnight, Uncle Rex," I say, kissing him on the cheek, too. I rub my breasts against his body, and touch his cock lightly, watching it grow larger immediately.

He sucks in a breath. "Callie..." he says quietly.

Dad is in the next room, so I whisper in his ear, "I've missed you so much. Come to my room tonight, Uncle Rex. I want to spend all night being fucked by you. My pussy is so wet and hungry for your big, hard cock." I look down to see his cock straining against his shorts. His jaw tightens, giving him an angry look. I flash him a smile, and walk to my room, putting an extra sway in my hips and humming a happy tune.

It's midnight. John is asleep. I know, because he snores so loudly, you can hear it all the way down the hall. I tried to sleep, but all I could think of was Callie. Nothing new, but yet it is.

Before I ever touched her, I dreamed about her often, and even jacked off frequently to thoughts of her. I knew it was wrong, but did it anyway. I figured it was just a little harmless fantasy. But now? Now I know what her mouth feels like on me, how hot and wet her tight little pussy is, and that she wants me in her bed. I know I want to fuck her more than I've ever wanted anything. I also know I can't do that, no matter how desperately I want to.

So, why am I standing outside her bedroom? Because I'm going to tell her that nothing more can happen between us, ever. That's the lie I tell myself, anyway. Deep down, I know that if I walk inside her room, nothing will stop me from having her.

I turn the doorknob quietly, then shut and lock the door behind me. Subconsciously, I know why I'm here. Callie is like a siren, luring me to my demise. I know it's wrong, but I can't fight it anymore. My need for her is too strong.

"Uncle Rex?" she whispers.

"It's me, baby doll." She smiles brightly. I clear my throat. "Look, Callie, I came here to tell you that nothing more can happen between us. It's wrong. Your father would be devastated."

She looks irritated for a few seconds, before changing into the seductress I saw a few days ago. "Is that really why you're here, Uncle Rex?" she whispers. "If it was, I think you would tell me during the day; not at midnight in my room with just the two of us. I think you want this just as much as I do."

"Fuck! You know I want this. You have no idea how much I want this. But baby, as much as I want this, it can't happen. I shouldn't have taken advantage of you before. You are young and don't know what you want."

"You didn't take advantage of me. I wanted you. I still want you. I loved every second of it. I may be young, but I know exactly what I want-you. I've always wanted you. And right now, I want you to fuck me. Please."

With that, she throws off her covers, revealing her gorgeous, naked body. Fuck me! All of her luscious curves are on display. She watches me while she squeezes her breasts. My cock has turned to stone again. I watch her and accept my fate, consequences by damned. I'm not strong enough to walk out of her room tonight without having her.

There's just enough moonlight coming through the window to illuminate her, making her look like an angel. I can see the folds of her pussy glistening with her arousal. Her large tits point toward the ceiling. Her pebbled nipples are begging for my mouth. She's the most beautiful thing I've ever seen, and she is all mine.

"Please, Uncle Rex."

Callie

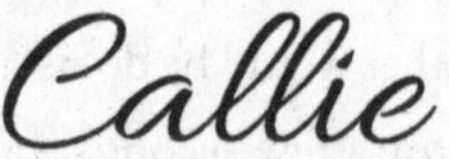

I'm spread wide open for him. I should feel nervous, but the way Rex looks at me makes me feel beautiful and desirable. He tosses aside the shorts he was wearing to reveal his fully aroused cock. It slaps against his stomach, leaking a stream of precum.

"I can't resist you, baby doll." He lies on top of me and kisses me; gently at first, then more demanding. He pushes himself down to the end of the bed. He gently kisses every inch of my body; my ankles, calves, and thighs. Just when I think he is going to lick me where I need it the most, he works his way back up my body, pressing kisses against my stomach before squeezing and suckling my breasts for what feels like an eternity. It's too much and not enough at the same time.

I arch off the bed, wanting more; wanting all of him. He kisses my neck before taking my mouth hungrily again. His tongue thrusts inside, dueling with mine, mimicking what he plans to do with my pussy. I wrap my arms around him as best as I can, pulling him closer. His hard cock rubs against the outside of my pussy, making me drip with desire.

"Let me taste you first, baby." He pulls me to his mouth and laps at my juices, moaning against me as I thrust against his mouth.

"Please. I need to come."

He pushes two fingers inside me while he sucks my clit. "Come for me, baby." I stifle the scream that leaves me as my body convulses, soaking his beard.

He lays his sexy body back on top of mine. He starts thrusting against me, harder and harder, until I can't take it anymore. I squeeze his huge biceps, begging for more. "Uncle Rex, please fuck me."

He sighs. "Baby doll, please don't call me that. It makes me feel like I'm doing something wrong. I'm not actually your uncle, you know."

"What do you want me to call you? Daddy?" He groans and his cock hardens even more. "Ooh. You like that. I like it, too."

"Fuck! Yeah, baby. I do like it. Call me Daddy. That's what I am to you now. I'll take care of all of your needs. Hold still, now. Daddy is gonna fuck your sweet little pussy until you can't move anymore." With that, he slams his thickness as far in as it will go. I feel a pinch of pain, but then only ecstasy. As wet as I am, he still has to thrust in and out of me several times before getting all of his thick inches inside me. He covers my screams with his hand.

"Are you okay, baby doll? I didn't mean to hurt you."

"Oh, Daddy, it only hurt for a second, but now it feels so good. Please fuck me with your big cock."

"Yes, baby. Take Daddy's big cock. Just like that. Such a good girl. Your sweet little cunt feels so good." He pinches my clit, sending me spiraling. He keeps fucking me harder through my orgasm. "That's it, baby. Come on my cock again." He sucks my nipples into his mouth.

"It feels so good," I whisper. "Fuck me harder."

He loses control, thrusting harder and harder until I can't take anymore. My eyes roll back in my head. The pleasure is almost too much to withstand. "Come for me, baby. Milk all the cum from my cock." His dirty words send me over the edge. He thrusts a few more times before he cries out and fills me with his seed.

Rex

I fill Callie's hot little cunt with my cum. I didn't even think to use a condom. I've never been bare in a woman in my life. With Callie, though, I hate the idea of anything coming between us. I let myself imagine her belly round with my child. The vision brings my cock back to full mast again. I hold her against me, breathing in her scent.

"Wow. Is sex always like that?" she asks quietly.

"No, baby. It's never like that. Never in all of my forty years on this earth. It's only that way with the two of us, and it always will be." I say, kissing her neck, and making her moan and rub her ass against my hard cock.

She flips over, smiling mischievously, squeezing her huge breasts and writhing on the bed. "That felt so good, Daddy. I want more. When can we do it again?"

"Baby, Daddy is gonna fuck your sweet little pussy all night long. I'm gonna fill you with my cum again and again until I put my baby in you."

Her eyes sparkle with happiness. "Yes! I want that so much!"

I know I should give her time to recover, but I can't help myself. Now that I've had her, I don't think I'll ever be able to let her go, no matter how wrong it is. I ease inside her, starting out a little slower this time.

"Don't be gentle. I loved it when you fucked me really hard. Fuck me like you want to."

"Oh, baby doll. I loved fucking you hard." I stop holding back and let myself go, slamming inside her again and again. I realize that we are being too loud, but can't bring myself to care.

I pause as I hear footsteps, followed by a knock at the door. Callie's eyes widen. Thankfully, I had the foresight to lock the door. John rattles the doorknob. "Dad?" she tries to say calmly as I continue fucking her quietly.

"I'm not gonna stop fucking your hot little pussy," I whisper quietly against her ear.

"Honey, I thought I heard you crying. Are you okay?" John asks.

I speed up my thrusts, enjoying distracting her. She has to really concentrate to make her voice come out normal. "Um, yes. I just, um, had a bad dream, but I'm, uh, fine. Goodnight, Dad," she manages as she orgasms again, biting down to keep from crying out.

"Okay. Goodnight, honey." As John's steps get further away, my thrusts get rougher and harder.

"You are so bad," she moans, smacking my shoulder.

"You feel so fucking good, baby doll. I'm already addicted to this hot little cunt. Even if he had walked in on us, I wouldn't have been able to stop fucking your sweet pussy," I say as I continue thrusting much harder than I should.

"Yes!" she cries as I fuck her harder, making her bed inch across the floor. She comes hard, squeezing the hell out of my cock, and taking me along with her.

———————————————

I wake up a few hours later to her riding my cock. "Damn, baby. You look so sexy riding my dick. Best wake up I've ever had," I say, thrusting up into her.

"You feel so good. I want to ride your big cock every day."

"Fuck, baby. That's all I want, too. I need to fuck you all day every day." I flip her onto her back, slamming my cock in her until we both come again. We lay there, boneless, for some time before falling back into a deep sleep.

I wake up the next morning with Callie wrapped around me. For the first time in a long time, I wake up with a big smile on my face. She is the perfect blend of innocent and seductress. She is everything I have ever wanted rolled into one perfect fucking package. Now that I've had her, I'm keeping her. I just have to figure out how to do that without both of our lives imploding.

Callie

The next morning, I wake briefly to Rex kissing me and telling me he has to go back to his room. "No! Don't go, Daddy," I pout.

"I have to, baby. We have to keep this a secret for now, but soon enough, everyone will know." He kisses me thoroughly before leaving the room. I fall back asleep for a few more hours. I am overly tired since I didn't get a lot of sleep last night. It was totally worth it, though. I just can't wait until we don't have to sneak around anymore.

Later that day, we have half the neighborhood over for a pool party. Dad loves to have pool parties and cook barbecue for the masses. He likes to have these parties at least once a month.

Rex and I try to blend in and keep some space between us. Every time I look at him, though, his eyes are devouring me. If he keeps this up, it's not going to take long for everyone to figure out what's happening between us.

I've seen a couple of the neighbor ladies hit on him already. Thankfully, he blew them off pretty easily. It's a good thing, because I'm liable to go kick some ass if any more of these bitches hit on my man. Believe me, I get it. He's sexy, but he's *mine*.

One of our neighbors, Jimmy, who's around my age, sits down and strikes up a conversation. He keeps leering at my breasts. It's fucking creepy. He's not even trying to hide it. I'm trying not to be rude, but I'm really not interested. I look up and see Rex clenching and unclenching his fists. He motions toward the cabana.

"Excuse me. I need to go to the restroom." I walk toward the cabana. As soon as I turn the corner, Rex pushes me against the wall, and kisses me within an inch of my life.

"What are you doing?" I manage to ask between kisses.

"Claiming what's mine," he says, almost angrily. He pushes my bottoms aside, thrusting his fingers inside me. "Fuck, baby. Always so fucking wet for Daddy," he whispers against my ear. He drops to his knees, and immediately devours my pussy with his mouth. His tongue thrusts inside me, over and over again.

"Oh, god." I cover my mouth to stifle my cries. Between Rex's magical tongue and the idea of someone catching us, I am so turned on right now. He makes me come on his mouth twice before standing back up. I struggle to catch my breath. "Wow. That was amazing! I guess we should go back to the party now?"

"Not yet, baby doll. I need to fuck your sweet pussy right now. I can't wait any longer." He pushes his trunks down. In one quick motion, he moves my bottoms to the side, picks me up, and slams me down hard on his cock.

It feels so good. I cry out before I catch myself. "Oh, god. I'm so sorry, Rex. We should stop. Someone probably heard me," I say, as he continues thrusting deep inside me.

He doesn't seem upset with me, and doesn't stop. "I'm not stopping, baby doll. I don't care if everyone hears you. I'm gonna keep fucking you hard until you come all over my cock. I tried not to give in to my obsession with you, but you unleashed the beast. Now you are mine, and I want the whole damn world to know it."

I hear footsteps, but I let him keep fucking me. I don't care who knows about us anymore. He feels so good. I need his cock so badly. I can't think about anything else right now except being fucked hard by my man. I look up to see Jimmy, looking shocked. Rex bares his teeth at him and growls.

"That's right, Jimmy. Callie is mine," he says, thrusting harder and harder. "She belongs to me. This gorgeous body and tight little cunt belong to me; no one else. Now, unless you want me to rip your fucking head off, I'd suggest you leave."

Jimmy turns around and walks out the gate. Rex looks me in the eyes. "You liked me claiming you in front of him, didn't you? I can feel your pussy getting even wetter."

"Yes, Rex."

He grabs my chin. "When I'm inside your pussy, you call me Daddy."

I look in his eyes. "Yes, Daddy. Please keep fucking me. Put your baby in me so everyone knows who I belong to." He growls and slams me down on his cock even harder, thrusting frantically, before we come together. Our juices mingle, rolling down our legs. He holds me for a few minutes before we decide to sneak around to the front of the house and clean ourselves up.

After cleaning up, we decide to watch movies together. We snuggle up on the couch and miss the rest of the party. I love being with Rex. I just don't know how much longer we can keep this a secret. We aren't exactly doing a bang-up job of being discreet.

I'm not sure how much longer we can keep this a secret. I know anytime I look at Callie, desire is written all over my face. It's not going to take long for someone to put two and two together. I can't keep my hands off of her; even at lunch.

Several of us are eating together at the local diner-me, Callie, John, and a couple of his buddies. I'm sitting next to her, and stroking her pussy through her damp panties. I shouldn't be doing something so risky, but I can't fucking help myself. I push a finger inside, and find her soaking wet. She keeps shifting from side to side. She needs me, and my cock is about to explode.

When I can't take it any longer, I tell them that we are going house hunting, then drag her out the front door of the restaurant. John has a puzzled look on his face, but he buys it. I help her into my truck. We drive for a few minutes in silence before I pull off onto a deserted dirt road.

I turn to her. "Callie, lay down and spread your legs for me. I need your pussy right now, baby doll."

"Yes!" she cries, lying down and tossing her panties aside. He tight little cunt glistens with her juices.

I push my shorts down, and thrust all the way inside her juicy warmth. "Fuck, baby. So fucking wet for me. You feel so good. Daddy could hardly get through lunch. I wanted to fuck you on top of the table so everyone would know you were mine." Our moans fill the cab of the truck. "I can't get enough of this hot little cunt. Gonna fuck you every day."

"Yes, Daddy!" she screams as my thrusts get harder and harder.

"Come on my cock, baby girl. Squeeze all of the cum out of me."

"Yes!" she screams before clamping down on my cock, drenching me in her juices. I slam inside her a few more times before spilling my seed. She is mine. I'm never letting her go.

Callie

♥

Once we clean up a bit and straighten our clothes, I am surprised to find out we are actually going to look at houses. "Are you sure you want me to go with you?"

"Of course, baby doll. You need to help me choose since you'll be living with me." He kisses me tenderly.

"Really? Does that mean that we won't have to be a secret anymore?"

"Not for much longer, baby girl. We just have to figure out how to break it to your dad."

We look at a few houses before we find "the one". It's a beautiful English cottage; something very uncommon in Florida. It has a chef's kitchen, huge bedrooms, and a gorgeous fenced yard. There's even a giant room that Rex plans to turn into a studio for me.

He fills out all the necessary paperwork, then asks for the keys. Even though we can't move in for a few weeks, he says that he needs to take some measurements and figure out where everything is going to go. As soon as the realtor leaves, though, Rex is on me. "Baby doll, Daddy is going to fuck you in every room in this house."

"Mmmm. Yes, Daddy," I moan, happily spreading my legs for him as he tears my panties off and thrusts inside me again. We spend several hours christening our new house.

Rex

I spend the night in Callie's room. I can't get enough of her. I'm in love with her, and want to make everything official. I decide to tell John about us tomorrow. I can predict how that's gonna go; not well. We have to come clean, though, because I can't live without her, and I can't keep sneaking around with her. Even if it means losing my best friend, I won't give her up. Ever.

I wake up from a deep sleep to a cacophony of noise outside. "What the fuck?" I look at the clock. It's only six in the morning. I look outside and see dozens of news vans. "Oh, shit."

"What is it, Rex?"

"I'm not sure, baby." I grab my phone off the charger. I had the ringer off. I am stunned to see dozens of missed calls and messages. I pull up ESPN, and there I am. Actually, there we are. A video of me fucking Callie outside, with parts strategically blurred. Under it reads *Former Dallas Cowboy Rex Cameron involved with a minor*? "Shit!"

"Oh my god!"

"Dammit, baby. I'm so fucking sorry. I should have been more careful. I just wanted you so much, I wasn't thinking straight. I should have known better. I never even thought about anyone taking video of us. Please forgive me."

She hugs me to her. "There's nothing to forgive. It's not your fault. I'm not even that upset about it, except for them saying I'm a minor." A pounding at the door interrupts us. "Oh, crap. I'm guessing that my dad *is* very upset about it, though."

John screams, "So help me God, Rex. You'd better open the door or I will bust it down before I beat the shit out of you!"

Callie hurriedly tosses a sleep shirt over her head. I pull on my shorts and open the door, not too surprised to be met with a punch to the jaw. I fall back against the bed. "Shit! That really fucking hurt," I say, rubbing my jaw.

Callie screams, "Stop, Dad! Let him go! I love him!"

I grin. "I love you, too, baby." I pull her into my arms, hugging her tightly.

That seems to take some of the wind out of John's sails. He sits down on the bed, looking defeated. "Why Callie? You're too old for her."

"Hell, John, I know that. But she doesn't think so, and that's all that matters. You know me, John. When's the last time you saw me with a woman? I'm not a playboy. I'm madly in love with your daughter." I pull her closer, kissing the top of her head. "We can talk more later. For now, both of you sit tight. I'm going to make a few calls and see if I can get this media nightmare straightened out."

An hour later, my lawyer and agent are holding a joint press conference on the front lawn. At the end of it, Callie and I walk out hand in hand so that I can make a statement.

"As my attorney has already informed you, this is a serious invasion of privacy that will not be tolerated, as well as slander."

A sports reporter I know yells out, "Who's the girl?"

"This is Callie Stevens, who is *twenty-two*. She is the love of my life and will soon be my wife. That's all I have to say for now. This is private property. Now, leave." I take Callie's hand, pulling her back inside.

She smiles up at me. "You told them that we were getting married."

"Of course, baby. I guess I didn't ask, though, did I?" She shakes her head. I get down on one knee and take her hand. "I love you with everything I have, baby doll. Please marry me."

She flings herself at me, raining kisses all over my face and laughing. "Yes, Daddy."

Callie

♥

Rex and I get married on Clearwater Beach a week later. We stand inside a heart of roses on the sand. I'm in a gorgeous strapless dress, and he's in a suit. It's just us, my dad, the minister, and photographer. It is beautiful and perfect, just like him. As we say our vows, we both have tears in our eyes.

Later that night, he helps me take off my wedding dress. "I'm so fucking glad to make this official. Now the whole world knows you are mine." He holds up his phone, showing me the official post on social media announcing our wedding. He tosses it aside, then kisses my neck, and down my chest.

He pushes the dress down, and admires my lingerie. "You are so fucking sexy, baby. You are the hottest bride in the world. Daddy is gonna fuck you so good." His fingers move my panties aside, diving into my wetness.

"Yes, Daddy. That feels so good," I moan as he strokes me.

"You are so good and wet for me. Your hot little cunt is always so ready for my cock," he says, fucking me harder with his fingers. He strums against my clit and I explode, gushing my completion.

"Yes, baby. Just like that." He rips my lingerie off and licks my seam. "Come all over my face, baby," he says, sucking hard on my clit, and making me explode again, drenching his beard with my cum.

"Now, you are gonna take Daddy's cock like a good girl."

"Yes!" I scream as he shoves his entire length in me.

He's a man possessed. He slams inside me deeper and deeper. "Fuck, baby. You feel so good. You are mine!"

"Yes! I am yours! Please, come inside me."

"Fuck, yeah, angel. I'm gonna come inside your sweet pussy and put a baby in you. Come with me, now."

I scream, as we come together. He fills me with his cum. He comes so much that it flows down my legs. The sheets are soaked with our combined juices. He gathers me to him, kissing me on top of the head.

"I love you so much, angel."

"I love you, too."

We don't leave our room for the next three days.

Epilogue 1–Rex

♥

Six weeks later...

I come through the door, ready to see my wife after a long day at work. I don't work full-time, but I keep plenty busy. I mainly check on my crews and make sure everything runs smoothly. I spend as much time as possible at home with Callie.

We turned a room in our house into a studio for her to work on her jewelry in. She spends hours a day doing what she loves, and her Etsy shop has grown by leaps and bounds in a short time. I couldn't be prouder.

Am I still obsessed with her? Hell, yes, I am. She's all I think about. I fuck her multiple times a day, and still can't get enough of her. I have a tracker on her phone so I always know where she is and vice versa. I can't stand to let her out of my sight.

"Baby doll, Daddy's home," I call out. "Callie?" Silence. She's usually in her studio or fixing something in the kitchen. It's really odd for her not to greet me when I get home.

I race up the stairs to our room and find her looking very pale and lying on the bathroom floor. "Baby, what's wrong?" I pull her into my arms, cradling her against me.

"Daddy, I don't feel good," she says, with tears rolling down her face. "I can't keep anything down."

A suspicion forms in my head as I look at her. "Anything else?"

"My breasts hurt, and I'm really tired all the time. Do you think there is something horribly wrong with me?"

I shake my head. "I don't think that's the problem at all. Baby, can you take a test for me?" She nods her head. I grab a pregnancy test out of the drawer. I have them at the ready for just such an occasion.

"You think I'm pregnant?" she whispers.

"Baby, you have all the symptoms. Plus, I have been trying to knock you up since the moment we got together."

She smiles. "Okay, but don't get your hopes up."

I give her privacy to pee on the little stick, then we wait together. We look at it after three minutes. It has a plus sign. I hug her to me, and feel moisture gather in my eyes. "Are you excited, baby?"

"Yes," she smiles at me with watery eyes. "Are you?"

"Baby, you have made me the happiest man in the world. I love you so very much. I can't wait for you to have our baby."

"I love you, too."

I'm married to a woman I love more than life itself, and now we are having a child. Life can't get any better than this.

Epilogue 2-Callie

♥

Ten years later...

"Happy Anniversary, baby," Rex says, kissing my neck.

"Happy Anniversary," I say before he takes my mouth roughly. I giggle. "You'd better stop. The kids will be here any time now."

"Not true. John picked them up from school. It's just the two of us for the next two days."

"Really? Dad is taking all three of them?"

"Yep. He was happy to. Now, be a good girl, and get on your hands and knees for Daddy."

I do as instructed, wiggling my ass at him for good measure. He tosses my skirt up and growls.

"No underwear, angel? You've been very naughty," he says, spanking me lightly and stroking his cock through his pants.

"Not yet, Daddy, but I want to be so naughty! I want to be fucked hard."

He quickly tosses his clothes off before bottoming out inside me in one deep thrust. We both moan. "Damn, angel. You feel so good."

"You do, too, but I need more. Deeper."

He grins. "You've got it, baby." He picks me up like I weigh nothing, and slams me down on his cock again and again until we both explode.

"Mmmm. That felt so good. Can we do it again?"

"Hell, yes. We aren't leaving this room for the next couple of days. Not until we can barely walk and I've knocked you up again."

True to his word, we stay in bed for forty-eight hours straight; only leaving the room for food, bathroom breaks, and showering. Nine months later, we have our fourth, and final, baby.

Our house is full of love, happiness, and a bit of mutual obsession. I love every minute of life with my sexy husband and wonderful children. We are so lucky to have found each other. We are equally obsessed with each other. I'm so glad Rex finally gave into his desires. I am so grateful every day to be happily married to the man of my dreams.

THE END

Taken by the CEO

Lacy Jane

Lacy Jane Publishing

Contents

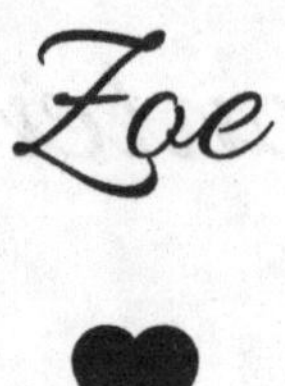

What the hell am I doing here? It's Saturday night, and I am with Cassie, my best friend in the world, scoping out guys at an upscale bar in the Four Season's Hotel in New York City. Why, you ask? Well, that would be because I am determined to lose my virginity. Tonight.

At the ripe old age of twenty-four, I'm still a virgin. It's not necessarily that I planned it that way. It's just kind of the way it worked out. I'm not opposed to sex; I just haven't met anyone I would actually want to have it with. I figured I had all the time in the world, but now, things have changed.

My parents are pushing me at their business partner, Whitney Covington III. Yes, he is every bit as pretentious and wussy as his name would suggest. They came up with an agreement where he would marry me, and then would pay my parents top dollar for their portion of the company so they could retire in luxury. Great idea, right? Yeah. No one consulted me. Like, at all.

It is absolutely ridiculous. I mean, in 2023, who doesn't get to pick their own husband? According to my parents, me, that's who. It should be simple to refuse them, but I am a people pleaser and hate disappointing my parents. Plus, they seem totally committed to the cause.

Just the idea of Whitney touching me makes me physically ill. Not only do I personally not find him attractive, but he also has a horrible personality. I have no idea why my parents got hooked up with him to begin with. Oh, yeah. Because he has tons of money. Old money. Like, Rockefeller money. I wish my parents cared more about my happiness than about making a big profit, but that's just not the case.

If I do end up married to Whitney, I'm sure sex will be something I'll suffer through as seldom as possible, not something I'll enjoy. In case I cave and marry him, I would like to experience full-blown passion with someone, just once in my life.

And that's how we ended up here. The idea is to find a sexy stranger and let him have his wicked way with me. It sounded like a great idea when I came up with it. It even sounded good while I was getting ready and putting on the very sexy black dress I'm wearing. Now that we're here, though, I'm feeling a lot less certain about it.

No one would ever accuse me of being a femme fatale. I'm way more likely to be curled up reading a romance novel or bingeing trash tv in my jammies than out partying. This is *so* not my scene. *What the hell was I thinking?*

"Maybe we should just go," I say quietly, looking around the upscale bar.

"Nuh-uh. Not a chance. Give it an hour. If you don't meet anyone who interests you, we'll go home and binge-watch reality shows." I give Cassie my best puppy dog eyes. "Sorry, Zoe. It's not gonna work this time. Girlfriend, I'm doing this for your own good. You need to get laid in the worst way, then tell your parents to shove it." I can't see myself doing that, but I love the idea of it.

We get some strawberry daiquiris and relax on a cushy velvet couch. After a few sips, I start to relax. "This place is really nice. And these daiquiris are delicious! " I exclaim.

"They'd better be for twenty bucks a pop." Yikes. On my meager salary filling in as an office temp, I won't be buying too many of them. In fact, buying one is going to put a strain on my very tight budget. It's probably just as well. I definitely need to have a clear head tonight.

We've been talking for a while when I look up and my breath catches. A man walks in that makes all others pale in comparison. He's huge; probably six and a half feet at least, with enough muscles to easily pass for a bouncer. He's not, though. He's way too well-dressed for that. I know enough about fashion to know that his suit is custom-made for his massive frame, and the Rolex he's wearing costs more than most cars do.

He's wealthy, for sure, but that's not what's so captivating about him. It's everything-his confidence as he scans the room, his square jaw and close cropped ebony hair, his piercing blue eyes, and the sexy scruff on his face that makes my girly parts stand up and take notice. Even his hands are sexy; so huge, just like the rest of him. I can imagine them doing all manner of dirty things to me. Plus, I bet he's big all over. Yum.

I'm so busy checking him out that I don't even realize he is doing the same to me until I look up and see those gorgeous sapphire eyes staring straight into my soul. Desire slams through my body, and moisture pools between my legs.

I'm paralyzed with nervousness as he walks toward me. I look over at Cassie with pleading eyes. She looks up, then checks out the Adonis walking toward us. "Damn! You go girl," she says where only I can hear. "I'll wait around to see what happens, but I'm guessing I'll be leaving without you. Good luck!" She winks and turns, walking back toward the bar.

"Wait!" I call, but she ignores me. I'm not the most outgoing of people, and I definitely don't know how to seduce a man who could give Henry Cavill a run for his money. *Fuck!* I'm so nervous, I don't know how to act. This was not a well-thought-out plan.

When he reaches me, I have to crane my neck to look up at him. When he opens his mouth, his baritone is just as sexy as the rest of him. "Hi there. I'm Julian, and you are the most stunning woman I've ever seen." Goosebumps break out all over my body and I melt into a puddle of goo. My nipples harden painfully at the sound of his voice. I just met him, but my body is already primed and ready for him. I am in major trouble.

Julian

♥

I scan the room for my lawyer and friend, Dan James, but he's lost to a throng of people. I'm about to leave when I spot a woman who takes my breath away. Let me rephrase-not *a* woman; *the* woman. *Mine!* The word circles around in my head. This is the one woman who is made just for me. I don't know how I know, but I do. I've never been more certain of anything in my life.

She's seated with a friend, and is thoroughly checking me out. The second I see her, my dick grows so hard, I can feel the teeth of my zipper digging into it. She's a beautiful little thing. She looks like Tinkerbell, come to life, but with enough generous curves to tempt a saint. She's the most gorgeous little pixie I've ever seen.

Her blonde waves frame her heart shaped face and flow just past her shoulders. When she finally locks eyes with me, her sky blue orbs widen comically and her puffy pink lips form an O. I can just picture my cock moving between her puffy lips.

I can see her breath increasing from here. This girl is mine. I know it. I just need to stake my claim on her without freaking her out. Proposing the second we meet would probably set off red flags. Slow and steady wins the race. I'll take things as slow as she needs me to, but mark my words, she will be mine. The sooner the better.

I reach her as soon as possible and introduce myself. The little pixie smiles up at me, blushing furiously. She is nervous. I like that. This isn't her normal routine. She's not a party girl who routinely picks up men. I would bet my company on it. She reaches out a hand to shake mine, and I lean down to kiss it. "And your name is?"

"Oh! I'm sorry. Zoe. I'm Zoe. I'm really nervous. It's just, well, I don't normally do things like this," she rambles adorably.

"Like what?"

"Pick up men in bars."

I sit down next to her, smiling. "Are you picking me up, Zoe?"

"Oh, god! No. I mean, not if you don't want me to," she stammers. "Just shoot me now," she mumbles, laying her face on the table. I laugh. She's fucking adorable.

"I think not. How about I buy you a drink instead, and we see where things go from there?"

"Okay. That sounds good. Thanks," she smiles shyly at me.

I need to remember to thank Dan for talking me into stopping by for a drink with him tonight. Otherwise, I wouldn't be sitting next to my soon-to-be wife.

I spend the next hour talking to my gorgeous little pixie. I finally get up the nerve to kiss her. I bend down and take her mouth with mine, gently at first. When she moans and returns my kiss with enthusiasm, I pull her against me and take her mouth passionately. I pull her even closer so that I can feel her sexy curves against me. Her vanilla scent is driving me crazy with desire.

I can taste the strawberry daiquiri on her tongue, plus something uniquely her. I kiss her repeatedly, running my hands all over her body. My cock is hard as a rock. I push her hips against mine, trying to get closer. When we finally pull apart, I realize that we got a little carried away. Thankfully, it is dim enough in here that I don't think anyone noticed.

I hug her against my chest. "You make me lose all sense of reality, little pixie," I say, kissing the top of her head. "I forgot we were in public. Hell, I forgot about everything but you. Look, I know that you don't know me, but I promise I'm not a player, and I don't normally pick up strangers in bars. I know that I've only known you for an hour, but I've never wanted anyone so much in my whole life. I would love to get a room and take you upstairs to continue this in private." She looks up at me with lust shining in her eyes. Her chest rises and falls with her deep breaths.

She nods her head and smiles. "I'd like that very much." *Thank God.* I give her a quick kiss and practically drag her from the room, making her giggle. I quickly secure a room for the night, and pull her into the elevator.

I push her against the wall and hold her against me, thrusting my cock against her pussy. "I'm going to make you mine, Zoe. Every inch of you will belong to me. This is going to be a night neither of us will ever forget."

Zoe

I can't believe I'm going to a hotel room with Julian, the incredibly sexy man I just met. If I had made a checklist for my dream lover, he would fit the bill perfectly. Sweet, check. Handsome, check. Built, check. Swoonworthy kisses, check. Sexy as hell, check and double check. This may be my one and only time to experience real soul-searing passion, like the kind you read about in romance novels.

We walk into the large room, but I barely see it before I am unceremoniously tossed onto the bed. "Strip, beautiful, or I will tear those clothes right off of you." I stand and do a slow striptease for him. I would usually feel way too self-conscious to do this, but the desire in Julian's eyes makes me feel confident and sexy.

Soon I am standing before him without anything on. His breathing is heavy, and his hardness is straining against the confines of his pants. "Fuck, you are so beautiful," he says, kissing my neck and making me moan. His hands roam over my curves, squeezing and heating up my skin.

"Thank you. So are you. Handsome, I mean," I manage to say. It's hard to concentrate. My skin burns everywhere his eyes and hands touch. "Aren't you going to get undressed, too?" I ask shyly. He holds my eyes as he slowly unbuttons his shirt and slides it off, revealing a mouthwatering chest. Heat pools between my legs as I take in his six pack, sexy chest, and huge biceps. "Wow."

He grins, and takes off his pants. His legs are thick and sturdy. Then he finally takes off his boxers, revealing his giant, pulsing cock. "Holy shit!" I say, staring at the forearm sized beast between his legs. He laughs, making me realize I said that out loud. "Julian, you're huge!"

"Thank you, sweetheart. Don't worry. You were made for me. Your pussy will fit my cock perfectly." I smile, nodding my head. "Lie back. Let me get you ready to take my big dick."

Oh, lord. His words are making me even hotter than I already was. I lie down. "What do you mean?" I ask, right before feeling his body pressing mine into the mattress. He kisses me hungrily, before slowly making his way down my body. He spends time massaging my breasts and sucking my nipples. I swear, I feel a corresponding ache between my legs with every suckle. "Oh, god! That feels incredible."

"Oh, sweetheart, you ain't seen nothing yet." He slides down, pushing my legs apart before devouring my pussy. "Fuck, little pixie. You are already soaking wet for me." He licks inside me, over and over, alternating with sucking my clit, and thrusting two of his big fingers inside my slick channel. I sob before exploding all over his face.

"Wow. I've never come that hard before," I say, trying to catch my breath.

"That's just the first time. You will come a hell of a lot more before the night is through. You taste so good, baby. I can't wait to be inside you."

"Yes, please." He kisses me as he lines his cock up against my sex and slams in hard, but only gets a few inches in. Even that much feels like I'm being split in two. He's a lot bigger than my battery operated boyfriend.

"Damn, sweetheart, you're really tight."

"Um, I probably should have mentioned that this is my first time," I mumble, trying to catch my breath from the invasion of his massive member.

He pauses, and looks into my eyes. "Are you serious, Zoe?" he asks, stroking my face gently. I nod, afraid that I've ruined everything. "Damn, baby. You're killing me. I love the idea of being your first, but this may hurt. I'm so sorry." He punches forward even harder, breaking through my barrier. He moans as I scream. "You feel so damn good. I'll try to give you time to adjust to me."

I can tell by his clenched jaw that he is having a tough time being still. I wipe a tear away. The pinch of pain that I felt is already gone, replaced by pure pleasure, and an ache unlike I've ever felt before. "Please move, Julian."

"My pleasure." He pulls out almost completely, before slamming all the way back in. My back arches and my eyes roll back in my head at his incredible sexual onslaught.

"Oh my god! That feels so good. More. Harder. Don't stop."

"Fuck, yes, baby. I don't think I could stop if the building was falling down around us." He pounds into me harder and harder, finally losing control. It should hurt, but instead it feels incredible. He hits my clit every time he thrusts. I finally let go and come hard. I scream as my orgasm sets off his. He moans out his completion as he fills me up with his hot, sticky fluid. It's everything I've ever imagined, and then some. It was only my first time, but I feel certain that I will never experience this much pleasure with anyone else.

Julian

♥

"I'm never letting you go," I whisper against her ear. She doesn't hear me, though. She has passed out from exhaustion. I should have been more gentle, but I couldn't help myself. I've never wanted anyone like this, and I've never been so out of control.

My parents have been happily married for forty-five years. As soon as they saw each other across a crowded room, that was it for them. They were married less than a month after meeting each other. They are still madly in love after all this time.

That's exactly how I felt when I saw Zoe. It was like I had found a piece of myself that had been missing. It's not just the sex, though it is fucking amazing. It's everything. I want to wake up every morning to her beautiful smile. I want to see her cheeks turn pink with embarrassment. I want to talk with her for hours and sleep with her in my arms every night. I want to see her belly round with my baby. I want everything she has to give for the rest of our lives.

After nodding off for a few hours, I wake up. The feel of her hot little body against mine has my cock standing at attention again. I thrust my fingers inside her pussy once more, getting her ready to take me again. She is already drenched and ready for me.

"Mmm. Yes, Julian," she moans, sleepily.

I thrust my hardness all the way in, causing us to both cry out. This time, I don't even try to be gentle. I fuck her hard, the way I have wanted to since I first laid eyes on her. "Zoe, you are mine."

"Yes!" she screams as I pound into her harder and harder. I pull her on top of me. She looks like a goddess with her huge breasts bouncing and her hair in disarray.

"Ride me, sweetheart." She smiles, and starts riding my dick like a champion. "That's right, baby. Get yourself off on my cock. Take what you need from me." After a few minutes, I help her by slamming her down harder until she milks all the cum from my body once again. I pull her against me and we both fall asleep almost instantly.

Later in the night, I take her again after waking up to her licking and sucking my cock like a lollipop. Seeing those puffy lips wrapped around my dick is the hottest thing I've ever seen. I know I should go easy on her since she was a virgin a few hours ago, but I can't help it. She is so damn sexy and responsive. I can't keep my hands off of her. I know that it will always be this way, no matter how many times I take her.

I flip her onto her stomach and pound her pussy with everything I have. "Yes, Julian!" she cries out. I pull her hair back with one hand as I squeeze a breast with the other.

"Mine, baby. You are mine. I'll never let you go." I flick her clit, making her come again. After several more thrusts, I finally give in, roaring out my release once more.

I stare down at Julian sleeping peacefully. Should I wake him? Last night was like something out of a dream. It was perfect. I've never felt so loved or wanted. What if he acts totally different in the light of day? I've heard so many horror stories about men kicking women out the second they are finished with them. The idea of sticking around long enough for Julian to wake up and unceremoniously toss me out on the sidewalk really doesn't hold any appeal for me.

Plus, let's be honest; I'm afraid. I thought I could just have sex with him and not get my feelings involved. I should have known better. I love the people I love very deeply, with all my heart and soul. I'm afraid that Julian has already managed to take up residence in my heart after just one night.

Despite his many declarations while he fucked me (quite spectacularly, I might add), I know that this was most likely a one time thing; a one night stand. The thought of that depresses me beyond belief, but I need to come to terms with the fact that there is no future for me and the ridiculously sexy man I spent last night with. Better to leave now with my dignity intact than to be kicked out in a few hours, bawling my eyes out.

I spend several minutes looking down at him, admiring his chiseled physique, and committing everything about him to memory. It will be what I think of in the many lonely years to come in my loveless, forced marriage to Whitney.

I finally force myself to go. I gently kiss his cheek, being careful not to wake him. "Goodbye, Julian," I whisper, "I'll never forget you. I love you." I rush out the door as tears start streaming down my face.

Julian

♥

A month later...

One month. A whole fucking month. That's how long it has been since I saw Zoe. After the best night of my life, I woke to find my soulmate gone. If it hadn't been for the scent of her and sex clinging to the sheets, I would have thought I dreamed the whole thing.

In the heat of the moment, I didn't even get her last name, nor did I give her mine. I've done everything I can think of to find her, but to no avail. I even managed to get the security footage of her leaving the hotel, but all it showed was her walking down the street and turning right toward the subway. She could have gone anywhere.

For the first week, I went back to the hotel bar every night, just waiting for her to show up again looking for me. After that, I gave up hope. I still pay a man to spend every evening there, though, just in case my little pixie shows up.

Zoe is a pretty uncommon name, right? I mean, how hard could it be to find her? A hell of a lot harder than you might think. Do you know how many Zoes there are in New York City? 289. That's a lot of people. And, of course, that's assuming she actually lives in New York City, and not one of the surrounding areas.

I've got a handful of private eyes trying to find her, but so far, no luck. Her friend paid for their drinks with cash, and no one else at the bar had ever seen either of them before. In New York City, the majority of people don't have a drivers license, so the DMV is out.

Hell, my mother is even on the case. When I confessed to her I had met "the one", she was ecstatic. She was ready to make wedding plans and pick out names for our children. When I explained the situation, though, she became a woman on a mission. If anyone can find Zoe, it will be her.

She is all I have focused on for the last month. I can't sleep for shit, I barely eat, I've lost weight, and I no longer care about running my company, Elliot Technologies. Work is the only thing I have focused on in years, but I have suddenly lost all interest in it.

I used to be a nice boss; I really did. Since Zoe walked out of my life, though, I have become a grumpy asshole who yells at everyone. My employees now cower and hide when they see me coming. I've even managed to run off three assistants this month with my grouchiness; a record for me. A little sprite of a girl has brought this CEO to his knees.

A knock at my office door brings me out of my thoughts. Carol Jameson, my right hand man, or woman, as it were, sticks her head inside the door. "Sir, Miss Cahill, your new assistant, is here."

Shit. That's the last thing I want to deal with right now, but I know I need help. I can't keep everything in my office running smoothly by myself. *I wonder how long this one will last?* I think bitterly. I walk to the door to introduce myself, and am stunned to see the woman who's been haunting my dreams for the last month.

"Mr. Elliot, I'm Zoe," she says, smiling, while she bends down to pick up her backpack she has dropped. When she looks up, her mouth drops open and her eyes widen comically. I grab her arm and tug her inside.

"Carol, cancel everything for the rest of the day," I bellow, before slamming the door in Carol's shocked face and locking it.

"Why did you leave?" I ask menacingly, backing Zoe up against the door. She just walked in, and my cock is already standing at attention to greet her. Just the memory of being balls deep in her sweet little cunt has me acting like a sex fiend. I inhale her vanilla scent. It takes every ounce of willpower I have not to toss her in the floor and have my way with her.

"I don't know. I've never had a one night stand before. I figured it would save us both the morning after awkwardness I've heard so much about. I just assumed that was what you would want."

I pick her up and plaster my body against hers. "If I had my way, we would still be in that hotel room. It never occurred to me that you would sneak out. We were never, I repeat, NEVER a one night stand. *You. Are. Mine.* How many times did I tell you that?" With that, I slam my mouth against hers, kissing her with all the pent up passion and despair of the last month.

I've imagined this so many times, I'm not totally convinced it isn't a dream. The last month has been miserable without Julian. I thought I was just a pathetic little former virgin who got too attached to the man who deflowered her. I ran off thinking that if I stayed, he would dismiss me without another thought, and it would have destroyed me.

Instead, I sneaked out and regretted it almost immediately. I have been so distraught, I haven't been my normal, cheery self at all. Everyone in my life has expressed concern for my well-being. Cassie has been worrying herself sick about me.

Every night, I dream of Julian, pleasuring myself while pretending it's him. Unfortunately, after having the real thing, my vibrator and tiny fingers are a poor substitute for his thick cock and big hands. No matter how hard I try, I can't make myself orgasm like he did.

Now that I'm finally here with him, I feel like I'm in a fantasy. He carries me to his desk, sweeping everything off of it. He quickly strips my clothes off of me and turns me over his knee. I am unprepared for the spanking he administers.

Smack! I squeak in shock as his hand slaps my bare butt cheek. Before I have a chance to recover, he slaps the other one. I am appalled at both his audacity and the fact that my pussy is now dripping wet from his punishment.

"That's for leaving. Do you know how miserable I've been? I have a man camped out nightly at that bar, just looking for you. I did everything I could think of to find you, but I still couldn't. Now that I've found you again, Zoe, I'm not letting you out of my sight. You are mine!"

He lays me down on the desk and laps at my pussy like a starving man. "I've missed this so fucking much. You taste so good, baby." He devours me; fucking me with his tongue and fingers. He brings me to the edge again and again before backing off, teasing me mercilessly.

"Julian, please!"

He licks his lips. "Damn, I love to hear you beg. I've dreamt of it for a month now." With that, he sucks on my clit, hard, sending me over the edge. "I'm addicted to you. I need to have your juices on my tongue every day to survive." I look up to see his face drenched. He throws his clothes off in a frenzy. "Now, I'm gonna fuck the hell out of your little pussy and remind you who you belong to."

Julian

♥

"**Y**es!" we both cry out as I sink into her wet heat.

"So tight. So good. That's it, Zoe. Take my big cock. Come all over it." She cries out as she comes hard almost as soon as I get inside her. I don't stop, though. I can't. I am out of control with desire for her. I fuck her through orgasm after orgasm until I can't fight it anymore. I cry out as I fill her with a month's worth of cum, praying that I just knocked her up.

"Oh my god," she says, trying to catch her breath. "What happens now?"

"We do that over and over until you realize that you belong to me."

She looks down for a minute before dressing in a hurry. She's about to bolt again, and I can't let that happen. I follow her lead and throw my clothes on, mainly because I'm not about to let her get away from me again, and I don't want to chase her bare-assed down the streets of New York.

"Julian, I would love to be with you, but I'm supposed to get married."

My head feels like it is going to explode. I slam my teeth together so hard, I'm surprised they don't crack. "You are engaged?" I say angrily, pulling her hand up and looking at her naked finger.

"Not exactly. It's not what you think."

"Have you fucked him?" I ask through gritted teeth, thinking of all the places I could dispose of his body.

"Ew! No! He's my parents' business partner. They are pressuring me to marry him as part of a business deal. I don't want to, but I don't really feel like I have much of a choice in the matter."

I put my hands on her shoulders. "There's always a choice, little pixie. This wedding to some other guy; not fucking happening; not now, not ever. The only person you are marrying is me. Grab your bag. Let's go."

Zoe

As soon as I grab my bag, I am slung over Julian's big, beefy shoulder. "What the hell? Where are you taking me? Are you kidnapping me?"

"Yes, sweetheart, I am. I'm taking you back to my evil lair until you realize that you belong with me. If you don't come to that realization, I'll just have to keep you there until you do." As we pass Carol, he says, "Cancel everything for the rest of the week. Something very important has come up."

Carol stares at us open-mouthed as Julian caries me out of the office. He's in such good shape, he's not even breathing hard. So unfair. I'm soon deposited into a snazzy looking sports car. He puts his hand on my knee and keeps it there for the entire ride.

While he drives, I turn to him and talk to him in a placating tone, like you would a small child. "Julian, you can't just go around kidnapping people Willy-Nilly, you know."

He has the gall to laugh. "Willy-Nilly? Really? You sound like someone out of a fifties sitcom. Zoe, you are my first and last kidnapping victim. Besides, once we are married, I don't think it will qualify as a kidnapping."

"Oh my god! You're just as bad as my parents! What about what I want? Are you going to force me to marry you?"

"No, baby. When we get married, it will be of your own free will. I will do everything in my power to give you everything you've ever wanted and make you happy. I plan to make the next several days so pleasurable, you'll be unable to live without me and won't be able to imagine being married to anyone else."

Well. That kind of took the wind out of my bitch sails. "And how do you propose to do that?"

"With every arsenal at my disposal. I am not above giving you so many orgasms you can't think straight and will agree to whatever I say." He grins like a mischievous boy. "I will do everything in my power to get what I want, Zoe. You. Forever."

I can't fight my smile. "Gosh, it sounds really awful. I don't know if I'll be able to handle all that torture."

"Oh, sweetheart. You will take everything I give you and beg for more."

Julian

♥

I've got her in my house. That's the first step. I talk a big game, but I would never make her do something against her will. I just have to convince her to stay. Forever. I know with everything I am that she is the one for me. I just have to make her understand that.

I show her to my bedroom. "I don't get my own room?"

I grin. "Nope. You will be spending every night in my bed with me."

She looks at me sassily. "What if I don't want to?"

I surprise her by kissing her hungrily. I stop when she is breathless and clinging to me. "I think we both know that's not the case." I decide to shift gears. She needs to know that this isn't just about sex for me. "What would you like to do with our day? Anything you want."

"Hmmm. How about taking a walk through Central Park? Is that allowed during my kidnapping?"

"Whatever you want, sweetheart."

A short time later, we are walking through the park. I can't remember the last time I've been here. For the last several years, I've lived and breathed work. Since meeting Zoe, it doesn't seem as important as before. The most important thing now is her and the family we are going to have.

We buy some bread so that we can feed the ducks. She tries to feed one duck at a time, laughing as several of them surround her. Before long, more and more of them crowd closer. "Help!" she squeaks. I pick her up and carry her away from the hungry duck mob. "My hero!" she says as I set her down. She pulls me down and kisses me, softly at first, then more passionately. We are both breathing heavily by the time we pull apart. I clasp her hand, then start walking with her close by my side.

The day is spent getting to know each other. I learn all about her family. She loves them, but they don't exactly sound warm and fuzzy. She is an only child, like me. I also learn about the wannabe fiance, Whitney. *Not fucking happening.* Her parents might not be thrilled, but tough shit. Zoe is mine. I'll destroy anyone who tries to take her from me.

I tell her stories about my childhood, and about my parents. I'm sure she'll be meeting them soon enough. I'm assuming Carol let my mom know what was happening, since the two of them are thick as thieves. Mom's been blowing up my phone with calls and texts since we left the office. I asked her to please give me a little time with Zoe before she overwhelms her with talk of grandchildren.

By the time we get back to my place, it's dinner time. I'm hungry, all right, but mainly for her. As soon as we walk inside, I push her against the wall and kiss her again. I lick her neck, then make my way down her body, kissing every beautiful inch. Goosebumps cover her porcelain skin. She strokes my arms and chest. I get impatient and rip her dress off, rather than unbuttoning it.

"Hey! My dress!"

"Don't worry, baby. I'll buy you another one." She's in a pair of sexy black lace panties with a matching bra. I strip them off her as quickly as possible. When she's finally naked, I lay her down on my couch, feasting on her soft breasts. I put my finger inside her slit and find her already drenched and ready for me. "Damn. You are always so wet for me, baby. Always so ready for my cock. I need to taste your cream again before I fuck you."

I move between her legs and take my time eating her sweet little cunt. She pushes my head against her. "That's right, baby. Get off on my face. Soak me with your cum." She tenses up and gushes her completion, crying out my name. I lick up as much as I can, not wanting to miss a drop.

"Julian, please."

"What do you want, sweetheart? Do you want to be fucked? Do you want my big cock inside you?"

"Yes!"

"You have to tell me. I want to hear the dirty words come out of your sweet little mouth," I say, teasing her hole with my fingers. I stop to strip off my clothes. My cock is hard as a rock and dripping precum. She looks down at it and squirms, trying to relieve the ache I'm causing. "I'm the only one who can make it better, baby. Just say the words. Tell me what you want, and I promise I will give it to you," I say, sucking on her hard nipples.

She squirms underneath me. "Please! Fuck me, Julian! I want you to fuck me with your big, hard cock."

"My pleasure," I say as I slam all the way inside her wet heat.

Zoe

"Yesss!" I scream as he slams inside me. Sex with him has become like a drug for me. I've officially gone from virgin to sex addict. Actually, just a Julian sex addict. It's all I can think about. I want him every second of the day. Let's face it, I've been a goner since the moment I laid eyes on him. "That feels so good, Julian." He feels amazing, and his sexy cologne is driving me insane, along with his mouth and hands.

"Fuck, baby. I've missed you so much. Missed this pussy so much. I'm gonna fuck you so good, every day and night, you'll never want to leave me again." He thrusts harder and faster. "Damn, baby. Your sweet little cunt is so tight." He stops for a moment.

"Julian, please!"

"What, baby? Do you want me to go slower? More gentle? Tell me what you want."

"Harder! Please! Don't hold back. I need all of you," I whisper.

"Need you, too, baby. So fucking much," he says as he starts thrusting vigorously. "Come for me, little pixie. Come all over my cock," he says, pinching my clit.

"Julian!" I scream as I come again.

"I'm not done with you yet, Zoe." He picks up the pace, thrusting even harder, causing the bed to move a bit. "Come again, sweetheart. Milk all the cream from my cock."

He grinds against my clit, hard, sending me spiraling once more. "Just like that, sweetheart. Your tight little pussy feels so good. Are you on anything, baby? Birth control?" I shake my head. "Good. I'm gonna come inside you now and knock you up."

"Oh, god!" His words make me orgasm once more, as he spills his seed inside me. I try to catch my breath. Wow.

"Come here, baby. Let me hold you." I snuggle against his side and collapse into a deep sleep.

I wake up and barely make it to the bathroom before throwing up repeatedly into the toilet. So gross. When I finally finish, I look up to see Julian above me, looking concerned.

"I'm so sorry you had to see that. So gross," I say as I brush my teeth and gargle mouth wash. He watches me like I'm a fascinating science experiment.

"Are you sick, baby?" he asks softly, rubbing my back.

"Yes. I'm so sorry. I should have said something. I've had this damn stomach bug for the last week or so. I thought I was over it, but I guess not. I've probably given it to you now." I hug him to me, apologizing again.

"Zoe, look at me," he says, raising my chin with his finger. "Have you ever considered that you might already be pregnant?"

"What? No! Absolutely not!"

He continues watching me while I think about it. I had a pack of condoms in my purse the night we met, but never even bothered to get them out. He comes closer, whispering in my ear and making goosebumps erupt all over my body. "We've never used protection, sweetheart. I took you several times that first night. I never asked about birth control and, frankly, didn't care since I planned on making you mine forever."

I realize that he could be right. I immediately go into full-on panic mode. "Oh my god! Oh my god!" I pace back and forth. "I'm freaking out!" I stop and look at him. He looks way too calm and happy. I thought men were supposed to be really pissed at unplanned pregnancies. "Why aren't you freaking out?"

"Baby, if you are pregnant, I'll be the happiest man in the world. You and a baby? It's everything I've ever wanted. I'll have my doctor come over and look at you right away."

A short time later, Dr. Sampson, a kindly older gentleman, runs my tests. "It's official. You are expecting!"

The doctor leaves after shaking hands with Julian, who is grinning from ear to ear. He hugs me tight, kissing the top of my head. "I'm so excited, baby. I can't wait."

After my initial freakout, I find that I am really happy about the little life inside of me, too. For the first time in a long time, I see the possibility of a future that I actually want with a man I love, rather than the dreadful, loveless one my parents have laid out for me.

Julian

♥

I'm riding a high after finding out that I got my woman pregnant on our first night together. I'm so fucking happy, I could burst. We are spending a great, relaxing day together when someone knocks on the door.

I go to answer it, only to find my mother on the other side with a huge basket of assorted breads and desserts. "Really, Mom? I thought you were going to give us a little time before you ambushed us."

She pushes her way inside. "Oh, nonsense. You've had some alone time and she's still here, so I'm assuming you've worked everything out?"

Just then, Zoe walks in and comes to a standstill. "Oh. I didn't realize you had company, Julian. I'll just go in the other room."

"Oh, no, dear," my mother says, racing toward her. "I'm Saundra Elliot; Julian's mother. He has told me so much about you. The poor thing was just beside himself for the last month without you." She gives Zoe a hug before dragging her into the living room to grill her. Zoe looks to me for guidance. I just shrug. My mom is a force to be reckoned with.

"How soon are you getting married? Do you want children? How soon will you have them?" Mom rapid fires so many questions at Zoe, she doesn't even get a chance to answer.

"Mom. Please give Zoe a little space."

"Oh, you are no fun, Julian. Though I must say, I loved hearing that you carried her out of your office. So romantic!" She turns back to Zoe. "It sounds just like something his father would do. In fact, one time..."

"Mom! Please! No sex stories about you and Dad. I'm already traumatized by the things I've seen and heard you guys do."

She laughs. "Oh, well. Now you can traumatize your own children."

Zoe looks at me questioningly. I know exactly what she wants to know. I nod my head and smile at her. "Actually, Mrs. Elliot..."

"Saundra. Or Mom, if you'd like," she smiles.

Zoe grins. "Saundra, we just found out that we are expecting."

My mother screams and hugs Zoe for several seconds while making a strange, high pitched squealing noise. "Oh my god! I am so happy!" She gives me a hug with tears streaming down her face. "I'm so excited! What wonderful news! I will give you two some time alone. I need to go shopping for the baby! Goodbye, Zoe. So lovely to meet you. I will see you very soon. Bye, Julian. I'm so happy for you! Ta-ta!" With that, hurricane Saundra leaves the house.

Zoe is bent over, laughing so hard she has tears rolling down her face. "Wow. Your mom is something."

I laugh. "Yes, she is."

"I really like her," she smiles at me.

"I'm glad, baby. She likes you, too."

"Do you really think so?"

I pull her into my arms. "Of course, I do. What's not to like? She knows I'm madly in love with you, and you've already got her first grandchild on the way. You might be taking my place as her favorite child."

She laughs. "I'm so glad you have a nice family."

"Me, too, baby. They're yours now, too."

Julian

♥

"**M**r. Elliot, it's the police. Open up," someone says loudly, while pounding on my front door. *What the hell?* I open the door to two young officers and a slimy looking fucker that I can only assume is none other than Whitney Covington III.

"Sir, Mr. Covington alleges that you kidnapped his fiancee, Zoe Cahill."

"That's preposterous! I assure you that Zoe came here with me of her own free will. Zoe, baby, come in here, please."

She walks in and takes my hand, smiling up at me. A calm seems to have come over her since she found out she is pregnant. She no longer feels like she has to do what's expected of her. "Ms. Cahill," the younger of the two starts, "are you with Mr. Elliot of your own accord?"

She grins up at me. "Absolutely."

"Are you sure, ma'am? Mr. Covington says you are his fiancee."

I growl. I actually fucking growl. No one is taking Zoe from me-not now, not ever. "She's mine, Covington; not yours. She is marrying me, not you. She is also pregnant with my child."

"He's lying! He must have threatened her! He's probably black-mailing her! She is not here willingly! She's supposed to marry me! I'll call the mayor!" he snivels.

The officers look at each other and sigh. "Ma'am, why don't you come with us down to the police station so we can make sure every-thing is on the up and up, and you aren't just saying this because you're being threatened?"

I pull her behind me, blocking her from their view. "Not a fucking chance."

"Julian," she says in her angelic voice while wrapping her arms around my neck. "Why don't you just show them?" She grins, biting her bottom lip. I look at her with confusion. She starts kissing and licking my neck. "Show them that I'm yours."

I grin and growl my agreement. "Are you sure, little pixie?"

She smiles. "Yes."

I take her mouth with mine, not holding back in the least. I'm always ready for her. There's no need for foreplay. Whitney needs to know once and for all that Zoe belongs to me. I reach under her skirt and find her already drenched for me. I undo my pants, push her up against the wall, move her panties aside, and thrust all the way in. We both cry out. I make sure the men can't see any part of Zoe that they shouldn't.

"Who do you belong to?" I ask, slamming inside her again and again.

"You! I belong to you!"

"That's right, baby. Every part of you belongs to me; no one else." I turn my head to glare at the three men. "Now get the fuck out of my house."

They leave without any further prompting. "Damn. Did you see the size of that thing?" One of them mutters. I hear Covington griping the whole way, but I don't care. I have Zoe. She is mine. That's all that matters.

"More, Julian!"

"Gladly." I fuck her hard, tearing her dress off so that I can suck on those gorgeous tits of hers. I feel her pussy fluttering before she convulses hard, taking me over the edge with her.

"I love you, Zoe."

Her smile is blinding. "I love you, too, Julian."

I go to the kitchen to grab the little blue box from its hiding place. I get down on one knee, and hear her gasp as I pop open the lid. "Baby, I bought this the day after I met you. I knew right away that you were the one for me. I love you so much, and I already love our baby. I can't be away from you again; not ever. I wouldn't survive. Please put me out of my misery and marry me."

She laughs, with tears rolling down her cheeks. "Yes!" she says, raining kisses all over my face. I grab her hand and put the stunning five carat diamond ring on her finger. "Oh, Julian, it's perfect."

"Just like you, baby. Just like you." I pick her up and carry her to the bedroom to celebrate our engagement.

"S o, are we planning to have a long engagement?" I ask, later that night.

"Hell, no! I'm gonna wife you up as soon as possible. What kind of wedding do you want? Big? Small? I don't care as long as it happens really soon."

"I honestly don't care. I just want to marry you. We can just go to the Justice of the Peace, if you like. I don't really care to have my parents there at the moment."

He hugs me close. "We don't have to have a big shindig, but I think we can come up with something better than the Justice of the Peace's office."

We end up deciding on Central Park. I mean, it's perfect. Right? I've spent the last three weeks running around like a lunatic, trying to pick out everything for the wedding. Saundra has been a huge help. I think she's as excited as I am. Julian hired a wedding planner and told me I didn't have to lift a finger, but who wants that? Like I told him, I only plan on getting married once, so I want to have everything exactly the way I want it.

Even my parents have come around. I know they will never be the warm and fuzzy parents that some people have, but they do love me in their own way. Despite not getting his way, Whitney ended up buying them out for a fair price, so they are now free to spend their time traveling the world, like they've always wanted. They are coming to our wedding first, though, along with a handful of other guests.

Julian's parents have welcomed me with with open arms. They are the best in-laws a girl could possible ask for. I know they will be wonderful grandparents.

Cassie straightens out my veil as I look at myself in the mirror. Wow. I feel like a princess in a fairy tale. Only instead of a prince, I'm getting a sexy CEO.

Since we found each other again, he is a much happier man. His staff is thrilled at the improvement in his disposition. He has cut back on his hours to spend more time with me. He ended up keeping me on as his assistant. It's a lot of fun, though sometimes we don't get as much done as we should. We have had some really great lunch breaks, let me tell you.

"Zoe, you look so pretty," Cassie says, wiping away a tear.

"Yes, she does!" Saundra agrees. She's crying, too. We've become very close in a really short time. She's like the mom I always wished I'd had.

"You two, don't do that to me! You know I'll start bawling with these damn pregnancy hormones!" I sniffle. A few seconds later, my dad is knocking at the door.

"Sweetheart? It's time."

Saundra hugs me, then goes to take her seat. I give Cassie a hug before she walks out in front of us. I give my dad a kiss on the cheek. "Are you sure about this, sweetheart?"

"Absolutely."

Julian

♥

I know that as long as I live, there are several moments in my life I
will never forget. This is one of them. As Zoe starts down the
aisle, I feel tears form in my eyes. My little pixie is stunning; easily
the most beautiful bride I've ever seen. I am the luckiest man in the
world.

Her white dress sparkles all over. It is low cut and form-fitting,
highlighting her scrumptious curves. She is wearing a tiara that Mom
gave her. Apparently, the whole thing is a Disney princess dress, since
she says she feels like we have a fairy tale love. I just know that she looks
stunning, and I'd do anything to make her happy.

Neither of us had any pre-wedding jitters. There are no doubts
from either of us. We both know we are meant to be.

When Zoe finally reaches me, her father gives me her hand, which
I kiss gently before tasting her sweet lips. "You look beautiful, baby."
She smiles up at me.

"Thank you. You look very handsome."

"Thank you, little pixie. Let's get this show on the road." She
giggles. The ceremony goes by in a blur, but I know that I will always
remember how beautiful Zoe looks right now and how much love I
feel for her.

When the minister pronounces us husband and wife, I kiss my little pixie until people start whistling and cat-calling. We grin at each other. I have never been so happy. My heart is overflowing with love for this woman.

"I love you, Mrs. Elliot. I can't wait to get you back to the hotel room," I whisper in her ear.

"I love you, too, Mr. Elliot. I can't wait."

Epilogue 1–Zoe

♥

Four months later...

We are waiting outside Dr. Francis' office for my ultrasound. Julian is freaked out because I am so flipping tired all the time, and the baby is apparently planning to be a soccer star by the amount of kicking he or she is doing in there.

He is such a nervous Nellie. It's actually really sweet, though. In fact, if I think about it too much, I'll start crying. Again. Ugh. Hormones. Anyway, he wants to make sure nothing is wrong. I've tried telling him that all pregnant women go through these things, but he always counters with some version of "all pregnant women aren't you."

I think he would wrap me in bubble wrap if he could get away with it. I mean, he's been over the top protective from day one, but my being pregnant has taken that to a whole other level.

As I lie back on the exam table, Julian squeezes my hand. The doctor comes in. I really like her. She's young and very up on all of the latest information on childbirth. Plus, it appeases Julian that a male doctor isn't touching me.

"Hello, Mr. & Mrs. Elliot. How is everything going?"

Julian proceeds to tell the poor woman more than anyone ever needed to know about my pregnancy, including all of the foods I have thrown up. Good lord. She laughs and winks at me.

"It's always tough on first time dads. Let's take a look and see what's going on with your little one." She starts moving the device over my belly as we all stare at the screen. "Everything looks great. Wait a minute. Oh, my. What do we have here?"

We both stare at the screen, waiting to see what she sees. "Is something wrong?" After a few seconds, I see the baby move and then..."Oh, shit. Is that what I think it is?"

"Congratulations! You are the soon-to-be parents of twins-a boy *and* a girl. I'll give you a few minutes to catch your breath and change."

The two of us just stare at each other for several seconds before we burst out laughing. "Did that really just happen?"

Julian grins. "Yes, baby, it did. I told you I wanted to knock you up from the moment I saw you. I guess I did a damn good job of it."

"Don't be so smug," I say, rolling my eyes at him. "Well, I guess it's good to know I'm not just being wimpy. I have not one, but two future soccer stars in my belly."

After we get over our initial shock, we are thrilled to be welcoming not one baby, but two.

Epilogue 2 - Julian

♥

Ten years later...

"Are you guys ready to go?" I yell up the stairs.

"Yes, Daddy, we're coming," Julia yells. Her twin brother, Zack is right behind her. Though twins, they look nothing alike. Zack is a carbon copy of me, and Julia looks just like her gorgeous mother. I will be fighting boys off with a stick in a few years.

As predicted, they are both soccer players. I'm not saying they are stars, but they are pretty fucking good. I could be a bit biased, though.

"Where's Mommy?"

"She's getting the little kids ready," Zack states, as if he's twenty-one, rather than nine.

I run upstairs to help her. "Hey, little pixie. You need some help?"

She smiles and gives me a quick kiss. "Yes, please. Zuri won't stop squirming long enough for me to get her dressed, and Joel has stripped his clothes off three times now. I laugh, and take off after Joel. He's only five, but he's destined to be a track star. He's faster and has more energy than the three other kids combined. I finally catch him. His little giggles warm my heart.

"Look, dude. We have to go to the soccer game now. Mommy will be upset with both of us if we're late. If you'll let me get you dressed and you stay dressed, we can go for ice cream after."

"Oh, yes! I'm getting dressed right now." He grabs his clothes and brings them to me. I help him get them on before sliding his feet into his shoes. I toss him over my shoulder and go check on Zoe and Zuri.

"Ready?"

She grins at me. "Ready. How on earth did you get him dressed so quick? You are a miracle worker."

I laugh. "Not really. I just bribed him with the promise of ice cream after the game."

"Well, crap. Why didn't I think of that?"

"Because you're not as devious as me."

She laughs and whispers against my ear. "I don't know, Julian. I've been thinking about all of the naughty things I'm going to do to you tonight once the kids are in bed."

I growl and kiss her sweet lips. "I can't wait, baby. I can't wait."

THE END

Forbidden Passion

Lacy Jane

Lacy Jane Publishing

Contents

I can't even remember the last time I was in my hometown of Cider Springs, Vermont. I came back once or twice after Mom died, but it's been at least five or six years, I would guess.

I've lived in Chicago for most of my adult life, but I've finally decided to slow down a bit. I sold my security company and my place in the city. I packed up my shit and headed home. I am planning to look for a house here and just work part-time as a security consultant. My life has been way too busy for too long. I need to stop and smell the roses.

I always knew that, eventually, I would move back here. It's so pretty, it looks like a postcard. Everyone knows everyone, and the crime rate is nonexistent. It's a great place to raise a family. We even have a big festival at Christmastime that people come to from all over. It looks like something out of a fucking Hallmark movie. Now all I need is to meet my soulmate.

Yeah. Not gonna happen. I've made it forty-five years without falling in love. I seriously doubt it will happen now. I head into the Fairview Hotel. It's the nicest hotel in town. It has been around for over a hundred years, and is stunning. I can live with staying here until I find something more permanent.

I look up and see my entire future flash before my eyes. In that moment, I know that my days as a single man are over. I always thought love at first sight was total horseshit. As I stare into the stunning eyes of my future wife, I'm thrilled to be proven wrong.

She's the most beautiful creature I've ever seen. She looks like an angel, but her curves would tempt a saint. My heart feels like it's pounding out of my chest, and all the blood in my body rushes south, making my slacks extremely uncomfortable.

She's fairly tall for a woman, but a good foot shorter than me. Ebony hair flows like silk down her back, and bounces with every step she takes. She's got on simple jeans and a t-shirt, but it looks better on her than an evening gown would on anyone else.

Her large breasts strain against the fabric of her low cut tee, revealing flawless porcelain skin, and her jeans look painted on her perfect, curvy ass. I'm so dumbfounded, all I can do is stare at the woman I know is meant to be mine.

She looks up at me and smiles. Her plush red lips open to reveal movie star white teeth, and her sapphire eyes dance with merriment and something else that I can only hope is interest.

I walk over and reach my hand down to shake hers. "Hello, beautiful. I'm Dylan Cromwell; your soon-to-be husband."

Jess

I've heard some unique pick up lines in my day, but this one takes the cake. I look up at Dylan. He is the definition of tall, dark, and handsome. He is the sexiest man I've ever seen. He is also fucking enormous. He is well over six and a half feet tall, and everything about him is large. His hand swallows mine and sends shivers down my spine.

His big muscles strain against his dress shirt, threatening to pop open buttons, while tattoos peek out from his rolled up sleeves and the top of his chest. I would love to see the rest of them. I've never given tattoos much thought one way or the other, but on him, they are scorching hot.

His short, dark hair is mussed, as if he runs his hands through it a lot, and his dark chocolate eyes twinkle as they catalog every inch of my curves. Just him looking me over has my body overheated and on the verge of orgasm. I can only imagine what he could do to me alone and naked.

I finally manage to look up at him and smile like my heart isn't flipping around in my chest. "Interesting pickup line. Do you use it on all the girls?"

"I swear to you, beautiful, I've never used that line before in my life. Now, how about you tell me my future wife's name?"

I laugh. "It's Jess Wilson. Very nice to meet you, Dylan Cromwell." He takes my hand and kisses the top of it, making my breath catch and my nipples harden. Damn, this man has me primed with desire and I've known him less than five minutes. I should be alarmed, but I'm way too turned on to care.

"It's very nice to meet you, angel."

"Why angel?"

"Because you are so perfect, you look like an angel. *My* angel." I smile and feel a blush hit my cheeks. He strokes my hair gently and sucks in a breath. "So fucking beautiful. Will you have a drink with me, Jess?"

I smile. "I would love that."

"How old are you, beautiful?"

"Twenty-five. How old are you?"

"Forty-five. Does that bother you?"

"Not at all. Does it bother you?"

"No, angel. I don't care about our age difference. Nothing will stop me from making you mine. Let's get a drink and get to know each other better."

Dylan

We start off with drinks, then move on to dinner. She's fucking perfect. Every inch of her turns me on. Her laugh, her smile, her obvious love for her dad, her independence, her intelligence, and, of course, her centerfold curves. I've been hard as I rock since I first laid eyes on her. On top of that, she smells delicious; like a decadent vanilla cake I want to devour. And believe me, I plan on devouring every inch of her.

I absorb every detail she tells me. I want to understand what makes this fascinating creature tick. "You mention your dad a lot. Is your mom not in the picture?"

"No. She and Dad had a brief fling in college. When she found out she was pregnant, she wanted to get an abortion. He insisted that he wanted to raise me, no matter how difficult it would be. He convinced her to give birth to me and sign away her parental rights."

"I'm so sorry, angel."

She smiles. "It's fine. Really, it is. I know I should be more interested in her, but it's hard to care about someone who didn't want you. My dad is a great father, so I never felt like I was missing out. On top of that, his parents helped us out a lot when I was little. They were the best. They were much older, though, and passed away a few years ago."

"I'm sorry, angel. It sounds like they were very special to you," I say, taking her hand and stroking it.

"They were. I was really lucky to have them in my life. I miss them every day. What about you? Family?"

"My sister and I were raised by a single mom. Unfortunately, she passed away from cancer several years ago."

"Oh, Dylan. I'm so sorry."

I smile. "She was a wonderful woman. She'd have loved you." Jess blushes. "Since she passed away, I've thrown myself into work more than ever. I finally decided I was sick of the rat race a few months ago. I sold my business and decided to move back to Cider Springs and work part-time. I may need to make even more of a change now, though."

"Why is that?" she asks, sucking in a quick breath.

"Because I've finally found the woman of my dreams, and need to spend plenty of time with her." I lean toward her and capture her lips in a gentle kiss. I feel her moan against my mouth as I taste her with my tongue. She is fucking delicious; strawberries, whipped cream and her own unique taste. I can't get enough.

I kiss her for several more minutes. I don't even realize that I've pulled her into my lap until she starts grinding against my throbbing erection. I try to take a calming breath, but it's rough. Even through her jeans, I can feel the heat of her pussy.

I've never been so out of control with anyone. I look around and realize we are the last people left in the restaurant. We have been talking for hours. The time with Jess has flown by. I'm not ready for this night to end, and I don't think she is, either.

I stroke her hair and look her straight in the eye. "I know this is extremely fast, Jess, but I'm not ready to say goodnight yet. Do you want to come upstairs with me?"

Her pupils dilate with desire as she bites her bottom lip. "I know I should say no, or at least play hard to get, but I don't want to play games. I'd love to go to your room with you."

I can't get her upstairs quickly enough. I take her hand and guide her to the elevator. I only allow myself to lightly touch her back. Anything more, and I'll lose control. I'm already holding on by a thread. I want to push her against the wall and kiss those luscious lips again. I know, though, that once I start, I won't stop until I'm balls deep inside of her sweet pussy.

I can hear her erratic breathing as she looks up at me nervously. If she backs out, I'll have the worst case of blue balls in history, but I will live with it. I'll do whatever it takes to make her happy. I'm in this for the long haul.

"We don't have to do anything, Angel. I can take you back downstairs right now if that's what you want."

She shakes her head. "No. That's not what I want. I want you. All of you," she says, squeezing my cock through my pants.

The elevator finally stops, thank god. My cock is so hard, it's painful. I grab her hand and we practically run down the hallway to my room, laughing all the way. Her giggles make me smile. I open the door, then push her against it as I close and lock it.

"Last chance to back out, angel."

"Not a chance."

"I'm gonna make you mine now. Once I have you, there's no going back."

"Yes, please."

Jess

♥

Dylan kisses me until I'm breathless. His kiss is hot and all-consuming; even more so than before. The door isn't the most comfortable against my back, but it grounds me. Otherwise, I would assume I was having the hottest dream ever with the sexiest man I've ever laid eyes on.

His lips kiss down my neck, sucking and nibbling. Goosebumps erupt all over my body and my panties are likely ruined, they are so wet. "So fucking beautiful." He kisses his way down my chest before tossing my t-shirt off of me. I would normally feel self-conscious about my curvy body, but the way he's looking at me makes me feel sexy and desirable.

He tosses my bra across the room and immediately sucks one of my hard nipples into his mouth while pinching the other. I hear myself moaning with pleasure as he squeezes and suckles my breasts. I'm already on the verge of an orgasm, and we've only just begun. He pushes his hardness against me, making me gasp and my pussy throb with need.

"Oh, god. You're huge, Dylan, and so hard," I moan while rubbing against him, trying to get even closer.

"Since I first laid eyes on you, angel. Nothing is going to help except being inside your hot little pussy." I feel wetness pool between my legs at his dirty talk. Everything he does makes me hot and bothered. I am burning up for him.

He helps me out of my jeans and shoes before leading me to the plush looking king-size bed in the middle of the room. "Lie back, baby. Let me get you ready to take my big cock."

I'm not sure what he means until he pulls me to the edge of the bed and immediately devours my needy pussy like a starving man. My back arches off the bed as he licks, sucks, and thrusts with his tongue and fingers until I'm a panting, drenched mess.

"Please, Dylan."

"What do you want, baby? Tell me," he stops what he's doing, apparently trying to torture me even more.

"Please let me come." I can't believe this crying, begging voice belongs to me. I've never been this way with anyone. I am a hot, horny mess, dying for what only this man can give me.

He resumes his torture, but concentrates his efforts on my clit. I'm so close. "That's it, baby. You're so delicious. I need you to come all over my face." That's all it takes to send me over the edge for several seconds. When I finally come back down to earth, I look up to see him swiftly undressing.

"Damn, you're hot," I think to myself, but apparently say out loud.

He smiles at me. "Glad you think so, angel. Right back at you. Hottest fucking woman I've ever seen." His complement warms me.

I try not to blink so as not to miss a moment of seeing every inch of his gorgeous body revealed to me. This man is twenty years older than me, but his body is in its prime. Tan skin, huge biceps, and a muscular chest with a dusting of dark hair that trails down to the part of him I want the most right now. I look at the sexy tattoos covering his chest, and can't wait to explore them in detail later.

He shoves his boxers and pants down in one motion, making my pussy pulse with longing. *Damn.* That beast is just as big as the rest of him, if not more so. It's supersized. "Umm. We might have a problem here."

"Why is that, beautiful?"

"I don't think that huge thing will fit inside me. It's too big."

He laughs. "I appreciate the compliment, baby, but don't worry. You were made for me. I'll ease into you, but I guarantee your pussy is made to take my cock. I'll be gentle at first, but soon you'll want me to pound into you hard."

With those sexy, dirty words, he thrusts several thick inches inside me. I arch off the bed once more, overwhelmed by intense pleasure. *Holy crap*! So, this is what all the fuss is about. I've only had sex twice before and, frankly, it kind of sucked. I thought maybe I just wasn't a very sexual person. With Dylan, though? I would gladly stay flat on my back, taking his monster cock all day long.

I feel a laugh go through him. "Glad to hear it, angel." I groan. I can't believe I just said that out loud. I apparently have no filter with him. I start worrying about saying more dumb things, but lose my train of thought when he starts thrusting harder. He's all the way inside me now, touching parts of me I never even knew existed.

"Fuck, you feel so good, angel. I want to live inside this tight, wet little pussy." He thrusts harder and harder, driving me over the edge again and again. His thrusts are rough and deep, and I love every second of it.

"Yes!" I yell. "You feel amazing. Please don't stop."

"There's nothing on earth that could stop me from fucking you right now, angel." He bites and licks my neck while driving me mad with desire. "So deep inside you. Wanna stay here forever fucking your hot, wet cunt."

His thrusts grow more erratic as he loses control. With every deep thrust, he hits my clit, making me come again and again. After a few minutes, I feel his cock growing even fuller, and know he's about to come inside me. There's no condom; nothing between us. I know in this moment that I want everything this man has to give, including his baby.

"Come for me one more time, Angel. I need to fill you with my seed." He pinches my clit, sending me spiraling once more. After several hard thrusts, I feel him fill me with his hot cum. There's an endless supply of it. It fills me up completely, then flows down my legs. He starts to move off of me, but I hold on tight. "Please stay just like this. I need you inside me."

"With pleasure, Angel. I'd happily stay inside you twenty-four seven."

Dylan

In the middle of the night, I wake up to Jess sucking and licking my cock. "Damn, baby. That feels so good. You need to stop, or I'm gonna come down your throat." Instead of stopping, she doubles her efforts, deepthroating me and sucking me like I'm her favorite treat.

Her hot, wet little mouth feels so good. I grab her head, driving my dick further into her throat, and making her gag. "Such a good girl. Take it, my angel. Take all of my big cock." With one more sweep of her lips, I explode, sending my cream down her throat.

"Fuck, angel. You are amazing."

She smiles at me and licks her lips. "And you are delicious." I pull her against my side and drift off to sleep once more.

I wake up early in the morning and see my beautiful girl lying next to me. She's so perfect, I can hardly believe she's real. I pull her closer until her leg is tossed over me and her hand is on my chest. The problem is that now I can feel her hot little cunt pressed against my hip, causing all the blood in my body to rush south once again. I have a feeling I'll be in a constant state of arousal for the rest of my life with this woman.

She stirs. "Dylan," she moans sleepily.

"Yes, baby?" I ask, kissing her deeply and caressing her body.

"You feel so good," she says, stroking my rock hard cock. She nibbles on my ear and neck. "Fuck me more," she says, opening her hungry eyes and licking her lips.

"My pleasure, angel." I sink into her sweet little pussy once again. I'm already on the edge. We are both extra needy this morning, and ravenous for each other. I'm a bit rougher with her than I was last night and, thankfully, she loves it. She screams her pleasure as I pound into her.

I flip her onto her hands and knees and slam into her from behind. At this angle, I'm even deeper. I can already feel my balls drawing up with my release. I thrust harder and pinch her clit, sending her spiraling once more as I fill her with my seed. She is mine! Now that I've claimed her, I'll never let her go.

After a quick nap and another round of sex (this time, in the shower), we get ready for the day. Thankfully, it's a Saturday, and neither of us has to be anywhere. We have breakfast, talking nonstop between bites. I feel like I've known Jess forever; I'm so comfortable with her already. She's like a piece of me I hadn't even realized was missing until I found it. I already know I can't go back to life without her.

When I told her I was going to marry her, I wasn't kidding. I'm about to drag her curvy ass to the nearest Justice of the Peace and put a ring on her finger before she can get away. I give her a long, deep kiss. "Marry me, baby."

She laughs. "Oh my gosh. You can't be serious. We haven't even known each other twenty-four hours yet."

"Fair enough, but I am deadly serious and I'm going to keep asking you until you finally say yes. I will wear you down eventually. That's a promise."

After a fun-filled day exploring the town together, we finally have to part ways. I'm supposed to catch up with an old friend of mine, and she has previous plans with her dad. We exchange numbers and make plans to meet up again tomorrow night. After all, this woman is my future. Nothing will stop me from making her mine permanently, sooner rather than later.

Jess

❤

"Jess! Where are you?" Dad bellows loud enough to wake the dead.

"I'm in my room, Dad. Jeez, you're loud." Sometimes I question my decision to continue living at home. I mean, I'm twenty-five years old, and I have my own bookkeeping business. I could have moved out a long time ago, but I haven't had any reason to. Now that I've met Dylan, though, I have a feeling I might need to do just that. We are definitely going to need some privacy.

"Sorry, sweetie. I know the two of us were supposed to go out to eat tonight, but an old friend of mine from school is in town, so I invited him over. I thought we could order some pizza and catch up. You're welcome to join us."

I scrunch my nose up. I would rather go see Dylan than some old guy I don't know, but he's tied up, so I might as well hang out with Dad and his friend. "Okay. But if it gets too boring, I'm out of here."

He laughs. "No problem."

I'm sitting with Dad in the living room when the doorbell rings. He goes to answer it and starts talking to his friend. Their voices are muffled, but chills run up and down my spine. The only other time that's ever happened was with Dylan. Weird. I walk in the other room to introduce myself to Dad's friend, and stop dead in my tracks.

"Dylan, this is my daughter, Jessica." Dylan and I stare at each other in shock for several seconds before I spring into action.

"So nice to meet you, Dylan," I say, shaking his hand.

"You, too, Jessica," he mumbles after several beats.

Dad goes in the kitchen to grab beers, giving us a few seconds alone.

"You're Dad's friend?"

"You're John's daughter? Shouldn't we just tell him?" he asks.

I nibble on my bottom lip, causing heat to flare in his eyes. "Maybe we should ease him into it. I'm not sure how well he's going to take it. I hate for him to get mad at you before you've even had a chance to reconnect."

"If that's what you want, angel, I'll do it, but I don't have any problem letting him know you are mine. I don't want to keep you a secret. I've already told you, I'm ready to claim you in front of the world."

"I know. Let's just give it a few days and wait for the perfect moment to tell him."

They go into the other room to catch up, but come back a short while later. "Guess what? Dylan is moving back to town and is going to stay with us for a week or two while he looks for a place to live. Isn't that great?"

I smile. "Great," I say, meeting Dylan's hungry eyes. I mean, I love the idea of him being here, but can we really keep our hands off each other for that long? We are playing with fire, and I really want to get burned.

Dylan

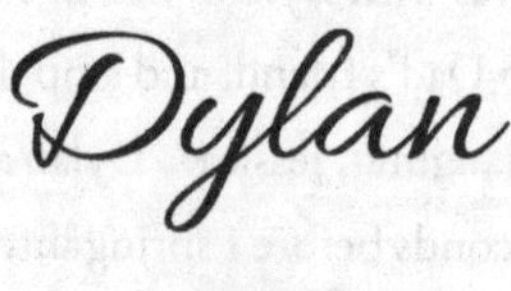

This is so fucked up. Jess is John's daughter. He's one of my oldest and dearest friends. I've known him since elementary school, for God's sake. He's a great guy, but somehow, I don't think he's going to love the idea of me fucking his daughter. When she said her last name was Wilson, it never even occurred to me that they could be related since it's such a common last name.

The three of us eat pizza, and laugh as John and I talk about the old days. I manage to sit beside Jess. Every time I have the opportunity, I discreetly stroke her leg under the table. When John is occupied in the kitchen for several minutes, I shove my fingers deep into her pussy, making her come almost immediately, right there at the dining table. She bites down on her hand to hold in her moan. She is just catching her breath when he comes back.

"Sweetie, are you okay?"

"I'm fine. Why?"

"You look really flushed."

Her face gets even redder. I try my best not to grin. Yeah. I did that to my little angel. I shouldn't be touching her right now, but I can't help myself. I'll be lucky if I make it through the next few days without throwing her down and fucking her in front of anyone and everyone.

I look at her as I lick her juices off my fingers. "Umm. Delicious," I say, truthfully. Her sweet and musky taste drives me wild. Her eyes go dark with desire. John thinks I'm talking about the pizza, but Jess knows the truth.

A few hours later, I'm lying in bed, trying to go to sleep. I know I need to stay in the guest room, but the urge to go to Jess is overwhelming. I finally get up, quietly opening my door. I walk down the hall to her room and turn the knob silently.

"Angel," I whisper. "Are you still awake?"

"Yes, but you shouldn't be here, Dylan. We are going to get caught." Her protest sounds weak at best, especially when her hips are already moving from side to side, tempting me even more.

"We'll be quiet, Angel. I don't think I can make it through the night without having you again. I need to feel your hot little cunt squeezing me." I can see her biting her lip in the near darkness, and know that she wants this just as much as I do. "Get on the floor, baby. I need to fuck you right now."

She scrambles to lie down on the floor, tossing off her nightgown to reveal her gorgeous, naked body. "Fuck, angel. You look sexier every time I see you." I lock her door and shove down my boxers. My dick is already hard as a rock, anticipating being inside her hot cunt again.

"Cover your mouth, Angel. We need to be quiet." I pull her legs onto my shoulders as I eat her pussy. I bite and lick until she screams into her hand. "Fuck, baby. You taste so good. You make me so hard. You are already so drenched for me. I'm gonna make you feel so good."

"Please," she whispers.

I thrust all the way in, sending her into an immediate orgasm. "That's right, baby. Come all over my big cock," I whisper against her ear as I thrust harder and faster. Her hips rise to meet mine again and again. "You feel so good, angel. I need you more than I need to breathe."

"Me, too," she whispers. "Harder, please, Dylan."

I sit down, pulling her on top of me. "Ride me, beautiful." She starts out hesitantly, but quickly finds her rhythm. She looks like a goddess riding my dick. Her head is thrown back, and she is lost in pleasure.

After a few minutes, I take control and bounce her on my cock, harder and harder, as I squeeze and suck her bountiful breasts. I finally lose control, picking her up and forcefully slamming her down on my cock again and again until we both come. After several seconds I carry her to her bed. I lie down and gather her close, stroking her hair. "I love you, angel."

She smiles. "I know it's way too fast, but I love you, too."

Jess

♥

I walk downstairs the next morning in time to catch part of the conversation Dylan and Dad are having. "It will be fun, buddy! I'm having a bunch of people over for the cookout. There are a lot of hot, single ladies in the neighborhood for you to meet."

Jealousy burns through me. Dylan is mine! I know I haven't publicly claimed him yet, but he's mine just the same. He is not getting set up with someone else. He's my future husband, dammit!

He gives an uncomfortable laugh. "I appreciate the gesture, John, but I'm already seeing someone."

"Well, if you haven't put a ring on her finger, then I'd say you're fair game."

I growl, about to go give them both what for, when my man says the magic words. "I'm planning to put a ring on it as soon as possible. I've already told her that. I'm madly in love with her. She's the one." I can't stop the goofy smile that takes over my face.

Dad takes a beat. "Wow. Never thought I'd see the day. That's great, buddy. I can't wait to meet her."

"Yep," he replies, looking at me as I walk into the room. We can't keep up this farce much longer. We really need to come clean with my dad. The longer we wait, the harder it's going to be.

The next day, Dad has what seems like the entire neighborhood over for a barbecue. Don't get me wrong; the neighbors are all very nice, but I'm not enjoying watching every available female (and even some that aren't) trying to hit on Dylan. Every female from early teens to late eighties seems to be vying for his attention.

I've also had some of the men hitting on me. I would already be pretty uncomfortable with that normally. With Dylan here, though? He looks like he's going to commit murder every time a man so much as looks in my direction. I have to say, I'm kind of enjoying his display of jealousy. I've never felt so wanted.

I walk to the side of the house to get a moment away from the crowd. Seconds later, a hand grabs me, pulling me into the storage shed. The sexy smell of his cologne and the fact that my panties immediately drench tell me exactly who it is.

"What are you doing, Dylan?" I ask breathlessly.

"Taking what's mine," he growls.

Dylan

I'm about to come unhinged. Watching every swinging dick in the fucking neighborhood talk to my woman? Unacceptable. I'm ready to lay claim to her, privately and publicly. I'd be more than happy to fuck her in front of everyone so there's no question as to who she belongs to. Instead, I am taking a moment alone with her so I don't beat the shit of out some poor bastard for merely looking at her.

I pull her against me, kissing her for several seconds. "You're mine!" I say, reaching under her dress and pushing her panties to the side. I shove my fingers inside her wetness, causing her to gasp. "Damn, angel. You're always so fucking wet for me." I spin her around and work my shorts down my legs. I bend her over a workbench before slamming my dick to the hilt inside her. We both moan as I pin her down and thrust harder and harder, staking my claim on her. "Fuck, baby. You feel so good. I need everyone to know you're mine."

"Yes!"

I thrust in and out of her wet heat, making sure she knows undoubtedly that she belongs to me. "Mine!" I thrust harder and deeper, playing with her clit at the same time. I'm out of control. The need to fuck her and breed her is all I can think about.

"So fucking perfect, baby. I need you to come on my big cock one more time so I can put my baby in you." Her pussy clenches hard around me. She cries out, as her pussy pulses and milks every last drop of cum from my body.

I hold her against me for a few minutes. I hate not being able to touch her in public. "Angel, you are mine. I need everyone to know we are together. We need to tell your dad as soon as possible."

"I know. Can we wait until tomorrow, please? I hate to ruin his barbecue."

I would rather do it today, but I agree. "No later, though."

"Deal." She reaches out her hand to shake on it.

"No, angel. You and I need to seal it with more than a handshake." I kiss her hungrily, and pull her against me again. Before long, I'm railing her against the wall. We won't be going back to the party anytime soon.

Jess

♥

"Where did you both go off to yesterday?" Dad asks. There's something strange about the way he asks the question that makes me think he might be onto us.

"We decided to go for a long walk," I say before I start in on the talk. We decided to tell Dad about us at breakfast. I'm so nervous. It's been just the two of us for so long. He has been my only parent for my entire life. I love him to death, and hate the thought of him being upset with me.

I also don't want to mess up the friendship between Dad and Dylan. I'm in love with him, though, so I need to act like an adult and own up to our relationship. I know Dad won't be thrilled at first, but, hopefully, he will come around in time.

I'm about to launch into it when he throws a monkey wrench in the works. "I have to run to the office for a bit. I'll be gone most of the day. Maybe you can entertain Dylan, Jess?"

"Sure," I say hesitantly. Something is off with Dad this morning, but I'm not sure what. He's acting really weird. He keeps looking between me and Dylan. Maybe it's just my guilty conscience making me imagine things.

After he leaves, I look at Dylan. He saunters toward me like a predator tracking his prey as we hear the car pull out of the drive. "Your dad is going to be gone all day, angel," he says, kissing a path down my neck. I nod my head, backing away from him. He looks so intense right now.

"It's been several hours since I fucked you, sweetheart. I need you to survive. I need to be inside you. No one else is here. We can be as loud as we want."

He pushes me down on the dining table, rips off my panties and shoves his tongue into my needy pussy. I'm already screaming with pleasure. I push his head closer as he works me with his fingers and tongue. He makes me scream again as I come all over his face. "Can't get enough of your delicious cream, angel."

After several minutes of devouring me, he pulls me up and carries me back to my bedroom. We don't even bother closing the door. We have all of our clothes off in record time.

"Need you so much, angel. Love you so much. Can't wait to make you my wife," he says as he kisses me and thrusts deep inside.

"Yes!" We both yell.

"Oh, Dylan. I'll be glad when we don't have to sneak around anymore."

"Me, too, baby. Me, too. Can't wait to move you in with me so we can do this whenever we want." We both stop talking as our passion carries us away. He knows exactly which spots to hit to drive me insane with desire. He pounds into me frantically, making my bed squeak so loudly, I'm afraid it might break. He squeezes my breasts and bites my nipples as I orgasm again and again. The pleasure he gives me is like nothing I've ever known. His thrusts are rough and completely out of control as he fills me with his seed, making me come once again.

We are still lying in each others arms, catching our breath several minutes later, when my door slams against the wall and all hell breaks loose.

Jess

"I knew it!" Dad screams as he lunges at Dylan.

"Dad, no!" I scream as he lands a hard punch to Dylan's face.

"Damn! That hurt. John, give me a chance to explain," Dylan says, ducking another punch as he grabs the sheet to cover himself.

"And you!" Dad shouts at me. "What are you doing acting like a little tramp?"

I scream as Dylan lands a hard punch to Dad's face. "John, you can disrespect me all you want. Hell, I even deserve it. But don't you ever, EVER, speak to Jess like that again."

Dad sighs. "You're right. I'm sorry, Jess. That was wrong. I was way out of line. I still think of you as my little girl. I had a feeling something was going on between you two. I really hoped I was wrong. I can't believe this shit is happening. How could you use my daughter this way?" he says, glaring at Dylan.

The two of them standing toe to toe is intimidating. They are both huge men, though Dylan is slightly bigger. They are both so muscular, and are seething with anger right now. Dylan stands strong, even though he is completely naked, except for the sheet wrapped around his waist.

"John, this isn't some fling. I met Jess before I came here. I haven't been seeing her long, but I'm in love with her. I have been since the moment I saw her. She's the woman I told you about the other night. I plan to make her my wife as soon as possible. I'm just waiting for her to say yes." I smile at Dylan.

Dad sucks in a deep breath. "What about you, sweetheart? How do you feel about him?"

I turn to Dylan. "I love him, too. So much. I can't wait to marry him."

Dad rolls his eyes. "Jesus. This is a lot to take in. I need some time. In the meantime, no more funny business in my house."

"Yes, sir." We both answer.

"And get dressed for Christ's sake. I don't need to see this shit."

He shuts the door, leaving us alone for a second. We look at each other. "Well...that could have gone worse, I suppose," I start out.

"It could have," Dylan says against my lips. "but I think we need to get married right away so that he knows my intentions are pure. What do you think?"

"I think I like the sound of that."

He pulls back and smiles at me. "Really? Is that a yes?"

I smile back. "It is definitely a yes."

"As soon as possible?"

"As soon as possible." He kisses me on the lips to seal the deal. We are interrupted by Dad pounding on the door.

"No more of that shit!" We both laugh as we get dressed.

Dylan

F or the next two weeks, Jess stays with me at the Fairview Hotel. It's easier that way. We both agree that we can't keep our hands off each other, so staying at John's any longer is out of the question.

We just need to pick out a place to live permanently. In the meantime, our wedding is set for this weekend. It has taken a lot of favors called in from a lot of people, but we managed to get everything set up for Jess's dream wedding in record time.

The day of our wedding is finally here. I know it seems way too fast to most people, but I know Jess is the one; no question. I want it official. First, I'll get my ring on her finger. After that, I'll work on putting my baby in her belly. She is mine. I need her tied to me in every way possible and want the world to know it.

John and Jess start walking down the aisle toward me. She's the most beautiful bride I've ever seen. She's always stunning, but right now, she looks more like an angel than ever in her sparkling white dress. She practically glows with happiness. When John hands her off to me, he whispers, "treat her right, or they'll never find your body."

"Yes, sir." I'd be worried, but I know I would never do anything to hurt my angel. I am madly in love with her, and always will be. I stare into her eyes as we say our vows, and realize for the millionth time what a lucky son of a bitch I am.

When the minister pronounces us husband and wife, I take my time kissing my new bride with all the passion I feel for her. When I finally stop, her eyes are glazed over with desire. I whisper against her ear, "We're spending thirty minutes, max, at the reception. After that, I'm taking you up to the room and fucking you until neither of us can move."

She smiles and licks her lips. "Yes, please, husband."

Jess

♥

Our wedding was everything I'd ever dreamed of. Now that it's over, though, all I care about is getting back to our room so I can be alone with my new husband. We mingle with everyone for a short time, then duck out of the reception as soon as possible.

I'm dying to feel him again. I can tell that Dylan is hanging on by a thread, and that turns me on even more. As soon as the elevator doors close behind us, he pushes me against the wall, claiming my mouth.

"Gonna fuck you so good, angel. Gonna make sure you know who you belong to, my beautiful wife."

"Yes!" He kisses down my chest before pushing the front of my dress down and sucking a nipple into his mouth, making me mewl with pleasure.

He pulls up my dress and shoves my panties aside, fingering my wet pussy. "So fucking wet. Dammit, baby. I fucking tried, I really did, but I can't wait any longer. I need to be inside you right now." He hits the emergency stop button, and pushes down his slacks as the elevator comes to a screeching halt. It all happens so fast. The next thing I know, he lifts up my dress and slams his cock all the way inside me.

"Oh my god! Yes. More, Dylan!" He lifts me up, impaling me on his thickness over and over again.

"You are mine!" He yells with each thrust. "My wife, my angel, my love." It feels so good. I never want it to end. He takes me so hard. He's not gentle, but I love it. I love to feel him so lost in his need for me. He fucks me for several minutes, until I feel him swelling inside me. His thrusts are even more out of control as he flicks my clit hard. "Come for me, angel. I need to feel you come all over my cock."

With that, I pulse around him and explode, pulling him along with me. He holds me in his arms for a few minutes while we catch our breath and try to fix our clothes and hair. We both laugh since it's pretty much a losing battle. We both look a mess.

He kisses me tenderly. When we finally collect ourselves, he starts the elevator again. This time, we make it to the hotel room, where he carries me over the threshold.

The sense of urgency isn't quite as bad now since we've taken the edge off. We manage to make it to the bed, where he spends the next several hours making love to me. He fulfills his promise. By the time he's done, we are both so exhausted that neither of us can move. *Best wedding night ever.*

Epilogue 1 - Dylan

❤

Two months later...

It took some time, but we finally found our dream house. It's a gorgeous English cottage that has plenty of room for a family. It even has a big office that the two of us share. We can't stand the idea of spending the whole day away from each other, so we both do our jobs from home as much as possible.

Another great thing about the house is the proximity to John's place. It's only a few miles away. That way, we have plenty of privacy, but can still see her dad whenever we want.

Things are much better between me and John these days. Even though he thinks I'm not good enough for Jess (let's face it, no one is), he knows I love her desperately, and would never hurt her.

She walks into the living room, and flashes me a tired smile. She gives me a quick kiss, then collapses onto the couch, laying her head in my lap.

"What's wrong, angel?"

"I don't know. I'm just so tired all the time. The littlest things wear me out, and I seem to need a nap every day. Maybe I just need some vitamins. Maybe I'm anemic or something. So tired. Need to sleep," she says, closing her eyes.

Damn. Now she's scaring me. There are lots of things it could be; most of them not good. "I'll get you a doctor's appointment right away, baby. We'll find out what's wrong." Thankfully, I have a friend who's a general practitioner nearby. He manages to get us in a few hours later.

After running several tests, Dr. Hoffman comes into the exam room, looking at both of us. I take Jess's hand in mine, kissing it. "Whatever it is, baby, we'll get through it together."

The doctor laughs. "I think you will at that. Nothing's wrong with you, Jess, other than the fact that you are pregnant. Congratulations!"

"What?" we both ask at once.

"About two months, give or take. I'll get you the information for a great OBGYN in town."

We are both still in shock as we leave the doctor's office a short time later. Jess looks at me. "Are you happy?"

I grin. It's finally sinking in. My baby is pregnant! "I'm over the fucking moon, angel. I've been trying to knock your sexy little ass up since I met you. Are you happy?"

"Yes," she smiles, though tears are rolling down her face.

"I hope those are happy tears."

She smiles. "The happiest. I love you."

"I love you, too, angel."

Epilogue 2 - Jess

♥

Several months later...

I am exhausted. After eight hours of hard labor, I swore that I'd never give birth again. I was ready to get my tubes tied right then and there. But after one look at little John's sweet face, I immediately forgot about all the pain and start planning on making another little one as soon as possible.

Dylan and I have been lying here watching him for the last few hours. He's so small and perfect. He is a mixture of both of us, with our dark hair, Dylan's tan skin, and my dark blue eyes.

"You did so good, angel," Dylan says while snuggling with me. "I don't know if I can handle watching you go through that again, though."

I smile at him. "I know it was rough, but look at what we made." Johnny stirs in his sleep, making us both smile. We named him John after my dad. He is over the moon about being a grandpa. The nursery is nearly overflowing with all the stuffed animals he has bought for the baby. Between my father and my husband, he will be spoiled rotten.

Dylan takes several pictures of him. He's been taking them since he came into the world a few hours ago. I never understood people taking a million pictures of their newborns, but now I get it. We have become those people.

"Maybe you're right, angel. The idea of knocking you up again really gets a rise out of me," he says, pushing my hand against his hardness. He's always hard for me, and I love it. The next several weeks will be tough for both of us. Our sex life is extremely active. Not being able to have sex for six weeks will be rough, but I'm sure we'll think of other things to do to each other to make it through.

"I love you so much, angel."

"I love you, too." My sexy husband and sweet baby are everything I've ever wanted. I can't wait for the next chapter of our lives to begin.

Epilogue 3-Dylan

♥

Nine years later...

"Happy anniversary, angel." My beautiful wife smiles at me.

"Happy anniversary. Dad just picked up the kids."

"I can't believe I've got you to myself for the whole weekend," I say as I rain soft kisses down her face and neck. "Whatever will I do with you?"

The ten years together have been all I could have dreamed of. I'm still head over heels in love with my beautiful angel, and she feels the same about me. We have five wonderful children. I wouldn't have minded more, but she finally put the kibosh on that. She decided five was plenty. I got a vasectomy after our last one, so we wouldn't have to worry about birth control.

Our lives are very full and extremely busy. The kids have lots of activities that have us running all over town. No matter what, though, we always make time for each other. John is great about watching the kids at least once or twice a month so we can have a date night. We sometimes plan something big, but more often than not, we end up staying at home and fucking each other until we are so tired we can't move. I have a feeling that may be what happens tonight.

"We've got dinner reservations, Jess. We should probably go," I say, kissing her softly.

She pulls away and smiles at me. "Is that really what you want to do tonight?" she asks, dropping her dress to reveal the sexiest fucking lingerie I've ever seen. The black lace barely covers her hard nipples and dripping pussy, but shows off her gorgeous curves in all the best ways.

"Fuck, baby. You are so gorgeous. Maybe I'll just eat you instead." I toss her on top of the dining table. "Mmm. My favorite meal." I move her tiny panties aside to reveal her drenched slit. I shove my tongue inside and immediately devour her. Her back is arched off the table as she thrashes and moans, begging for more. I push three fingers inside her as I suck on her clit. She detonates immediately, drenching my face in her juices.

Once she is boneless, I pick her up and carry her to the bedroom. I toss her on the bed and quickly strip my clothes off, squeezing my cock hard to get it under control. I'm already dripping precum for my sweet angel.

"Are you ready for this, angel?"

"So fucking ready," she says as I climb on top of her and thrust all the way in.

"Fuck, baby. Ten years and I still can't get enough of you."

"Me, too," she breathes against my neck. "Harder, Dylan. Fuck me harder."

"As you wish, beautiful." I let myself go, giving us both what we want. We generally have to keep the noise level down. With no one home, though, all bets are off. We can be as loud as we want. The headboard slams against the wall as I pound my dick into my gorgeous wife. After a few minutes, we are both out of control.

"Come for me one more time, angel," I say, pinching her clit. She screams, exploding and pulsing around my hard cock. I let go and come so hard, I nearly black out. Fucking my angel is my addiction; one that I never plan to stop. It gets better every time.

I hold her against me. "We'd better rest up, angel. We have a long weekend alone and I intend to make the most of it."

She smiles. "Sounds perfect. Love you, Dylan," she says, kissing me then settling against my chest.

"Love you, too, angel. So fucking much."

THE END

The Guardian's Temptation

Lacy Jane

Lacy Jane Publishing

Contents

Ryder

I'm going to hell. I stroke my cock while I watch Nichole on my computer. She's my dream girl, my ward, and my fucking obsession. I know it's wrong to watch her, but I can't help myself. I stroke myself harder as I watch her flit from room to room, and imagine taking her beautiful body in every position imaginable. Just that is enough to send me over the edge in minutes. I clean up the mess I've made and return to watching her.

I have cameras all over our house. I put them in several months ago. I managed to stop myself from putting them in her bedroom and bathroom, but that's it. Anywhere else in the house she goes, I can watch her every move. And watch her, I do. I like to think it keeps me from doing something I shouldn't, like throwing her down on the bed and fucking her till neither of us can move.

It's wrong. I do realize that, but I'm addicted to her and this is how I feed my addiction without losing control. I don't smoke, drink, or do drugs. My only addiction is her. I have to be able to see her at all times. She has no idea that I spend hours every day in my office at work and in my home office watching her on my computer. I have for months. I jack off every night watching her, and often during the day, too. I have even gone into her room and watched her sleep. I've gotten myself off watching her and spread my cum all over her gorgeous body.

She smiles as she finishes up some work on her computer. Watching her smile is like watching the sun rise; it lights up the whole world. She is so fucking gorgeous. She's my everything. She's the object of my every desire; my total obsession. I've done my best to make sure she has no idea how gone I am for her.

The dirty things I picture doing to her are so wrong, but I can't stop the filthy thoughts going through my head. Why don't I do something about it? Because not only is she almost half my age, but I'm her fucking guardian to boot, making her completely and utterly off limits to me.

It's not as bad as it sounds, really. At least, I like to think so. I'm not technically her guardian anymore since she's an adult, but I've raised her since she was thirteen, and am the only parental figure left in her life.

Her dad, Lenny and I had been best friends for our entire lives. We were next door neighbors and grew up together. Right after we graduated from high school, Lenny's girlfriend, Sherry, got pregnant unexpectedly. She had no interest in having a child, but Lenny convinced her to have the baby and sign her parental rights over to him.

Right after Nichole was born, he named me her guardian if anything ever happened to him. I was touched and flattered, but never dreamed I would ever have to raise her. When Lenny passed away after an extremely short battle with cancer, Nichole became my responsibility.

When Lenny died, I did everything I could to make things easier for Nichole, while trying to grieve myself. It took a bit, but we finally got into a rhythm and routine. We had a new normal, and it worked for us. We hung out together, took trips, played games, watched movies;

all the normal stuff a family does. She became the most important person in my life.

She is so incredibly smart. After graduating Valedictorian of her high school class, she went off to college at MIT. I was thrilled for her, but felt an emptiness without her here. Since our home in Cedar Falls, Montana is so far from Boston, she made it back for holidays, but only a few times a year. She had internships every summer, so I didn't get to see her then, either.

When she graduated with her degree in computer science nine months ago, she moved back in and started freelancing in cybersecurity. She was already in high demand and could have gotten her own place, but I was thrilled she decided to come back home instead. I had missed her terribly.

It was during her senior year in college when my feelings for her changed. When she came home on one of her visits, she gave me a hug and my cock immediately turned to stone. I was stunned because that had never happened before; not with her or anyone else. I was appalled and had hoped it was a one-time thing, but nope. Every time she has come near me since, my body has immediately gone on high alert. She's the only woman I have ever reacted so strongly to.

Even though I shouldn't, I live for her hugs and kisses. I will gladly take any excuse to touch her. I just have to keep enough distance between us that she doesn't find out what a pervert I really am for her.

I always thought she was adorable, but I'd never really noticed what a gorgeous woman she had become. Now, at twenty-two, her curvy little body drives me insane, and I can't look at her long, ebony hair without imagining fisting it while pumping my cock inside her. Her pale, creamy skin is flawless, and her heavy breasts and full hips are perfect for fucking and having my babies.

Her puffy pink lips play a starring role in my fantasies, but I also love seeing her gorgeous jade eyes twinkle with happiness. Her scent drives me insane-vanilla and strawberries. She smells so fucking delicious, I want to eat her up. Even the little smattering of freckles across her nose is adorable. Everything about her turns me the fuck on.

Besides everything else, she is the sweetest woman alive. She is kind to everyone, and everybody loves her. She takes good care of me. I take care of her, too, but I often want to in ways I shouldn't.

I spend every second of every day thinking of her and all the dirty things I want to do to her. I'm fucking obsessed with her. Every time a male so much as glances at her, I want to beat the shit out of him. I've scared off plenty of potential suitors; believe me. That's normal, right? Just a guardian's natural reaction, trying to protect his ward. At least, that's what I keep telling myself. What probably isn't a normal reaction? Having a cock that's hard enough to cut through concrete every time he sees his ward, or even thinks about her.

It's a major fucking problem. That's why I've tried to spend less time with her since she came back home. I know she feels neglected, but she hasn't said anything. I'm sure she doesn't want me to feel guilty. I want to be with her more than anything, but I don't trust myself around her.

I do my best, but the temptation to touch her is just too strong. Whenever we watch a movie, she snuggles up against me, turning my cock to stone, and making me forget all the reasons touching her is a really, really bad idea. It takes every ounce of my self-control to keep my hands to myself. Every. Fucking. Time. If I'm close to her, at some point, my control will snap, and I will claim her. If that happens, I know that I will never be able to let her go.

Nichole

♥

"Goodnight, Uncle Ryder," I whisper, taking the opportunity to hug him close and kiss his cheek. *Damn, he smells delicious!* He smells like his yummy cologne and a sexy scent that is his alone. I swiped a bottle of his cologne a long time ago. I spray it on my pillow every night and pretend it's him. Pathetic, right?

My hands squeeze his biceps as he holds me. My nipples stiffen and my panties soak just from being this close to him. I love when he holds me close. I'm pretty sure he sniffs my hair before grumbling and racing to his bedroom. *Damn!* It's the first time I've seen him in days, and I only got to see him for a few minutes. It makes me so sad. He's never home anymore. I miss him so much. I hope he doesn't have a girlfriend. Just the idea of him with another woman makes me nauseous.

I huff as I throw myself on top of my comforter. I don't know anything about seducing a man, but I recognize that it's damn near impossible if the two of you are never even in the same place. Ryder has always spent lots of time with me, but since I moved back in, he has avoided me like the plague. It's like he knows the dirty, dirty thoughts going through my head and doesn't want to encourage them.

I've been trying my best to get him to notice me as a woman since I moved back in. I get that the whole guardian thing makes it a little weird, but it doesn't bother me at all. I mean, who cares? He is the most important person in my life. I'm a grown-ass woman now; not a little kid. I am desperate for him to make a move on me, but that hasn't happened.

Sometimes, it seems like he's interested, but my radar could be way off. My experience with men is non-existent, after all. Maybe it's just wishful thinking on my part. He might still see me as a little kid. I swear, though, sometimes I catch him sniffing my hair or looking at me like I'm a tasty treat he wants to devour. I live for those moments.

I want him so much. I spend every night having lustful fantasies about him. I've pictured him kissing and fucking me so many times, it's sometimes hard to remember it hasn't really happened-yet. I'm determined to make sure it does. If I had a vision board, it would be covered with pictures of Ryder, and a wedding and babies.

It's not just physical, though. I love him with all my heart. He can be gruff and growly, but he is a good, good man. He took me in during the most difficult time of my life, and became my rock. No matter what I needed, he was always there. He held me while I cried, and has always been my biggest cheerleader.

I've been in love with him for as long as I can remember. Even when I was a kid, I thought he was so handsome. His sweet smile and huge, tattooed muscles did it for me then, and they totally do it for me now. That dark hair and deep blue eyes, along with the scruff on his face? Yum. So fucking sexy. I idolized him. No other boy or man could ever compare to his perfection.

For years, I wrote it off as a childhood crush; something that would eventually go away. It hasn't, though. Gone away, that is. It has only gotten stronger, hotter, and dirtier. Every time I came home from college to visit, I thought that maybe I would feel nothing but familial love toward Ryder, but that wasn't the case.

I had hoped that I'd think my crush on him had been silly, but, instead, it just got worse. Whenever I got close to him, my pussy would pulse with need and my nipples would pebble. Why did I want him so badly? He was just a man, after all.

He's not, though. He's the hottest fucking man on the planet. He has a face that movie stars would kill for, and thick, dark hair I'd love to run my fingers through. He has huge hands that I long to feel caressing my body, and a physique that is so incredibly ripped, he has actually been approached by gym owners, wanting him to be in their ads.

From his tree trunk sized thighs to his massive biceps to his sexy, tattooed torso, he is flawless. He is one hundred percent smoking hot man. I spend way too much time imagining his body pressed against mine as I run my hands over every inch of his huge, muscular body.

My need for him was bad enough already, but after what I saw last week? Yikes. It's been off the charts ever since then. I let myself remember that night in detail…

I'm downstairs, getting a midnight snack when I hear Ryder swimming laps. I glance at the pool room, only to find myself mesmerized by the gorgeous sight in front of me.

He is swimming naked. Totally naked. All six foot plus of his gorgeous muscles are on display for my viewing pleasure. I wish I had my phone with me so I could video this. I watch his muscles ripple with every stroke through the water. Damn, his arms and back are so jacked! His firm, sexy ass is in my line of sight, too. Only his cock is hidden from my view. I would love to see what it looks like. It's probably not as big as I'm imagining, though. I'm sure it's just a run of the mill, average-sized cock. Surely something about this man isn't perfect.

*He steps out of the water and I nearly choke as I realize that no, I was **way** off base. He has a porn god sized dick. It's thick, ridged, angry looking, and steadily dripping precum. It's hard as a rock, and standing straight up, reaching past his belly button. He closes his eyes and strokes it a few times and moans, causing moisture to instantly pool between my legs. I hold my breath as I watch him jack his monster cock off.*

When I see cum shoot out of it, I gasp as my own orgasm takes me by surprise. I take a few seconds to catch my breath. He looks toward me, but, thankfully, I'm hidden from view. I manage to gather myself and sneak back to my room without him seeing me. Imagining him totally naked is one thing, literally seeing him in the flesh is quite another. That was the sexiest thing I've ever seen-better than any porn out there.

I spend a long time that night with my vibrator, picturing Ryder's incredible cock and gorgeous body, but nothing soothes the ache between my legs. Nothing will, until I finally have him there.

Just thinking about that night fuels my never-ending sex fantasies about him. Why didn't I just go out there and climb his naked body like a tree? He probably would have pushed me away, but what if he hadn't? What if he'd thrown me down and taken me like a hungry animal? I wasted a golden opportunity, but, believe me, if I see him like that again, I will make the most of it. I want him so much. I will use every tool in my arsenal to make him mine.

Nichole

♥

"Hey, sweetheart," Ryder greets me. I run into his arms, hugging him hard. I've missed him so much. I hate that he's never around anymore.

"I miss you, you know."

"I miss you, too, baby girl. How about I order us some Chinese food and we spend the night playing games?"

"Yes!" I jump up and down, clapping. "I'd love that." I love it when we play games. I can't even remember the last time we did that together; probably when I was still in college.

A short time later, we have finished off way too much Chinese food and are playing Yahtzee. After I wax him in that game, we move on to poker. We play several hands before I try to up the stakes. It's late, and I'm feeling warm as I remember seeing him naked. It's kind of hard to erase that memory from my head. I would love to see him again, up close and personal.

I grin at him, suddenly struck by inspiration. "Why don't we play strip poker?" He is in the middle of taking a drink, and starts choking. "Oh my gosh! Are you okay?" I ask, slapping his back to try and help.

He finally gets his coughing under control. "I'm okay, baby girl, but it's late. I should probably go on to bed."

"No strip poker?"

His eyes dilate and he sucks in a breath, staring at me for several beats with something akin to hunger. He shakes his head. "No strip poker, sweetheart. Goodnight," he says, kissing the top of my head and walking to his room. *Damn!* I'll have to try a different tactic. I need to regroup and think of something else. Maybe the best approach is a direct one.

Ryder

♥

"Uncle Ryder! I'm so glad to see you."

Nichole greets me with a hug and a quick kiss on the mouth. I try my best not to notice how little clothing she has on tonight. She would still be a walking temptation, even in a potato sack, but right now, her choice of clothing is threatening my composure.

Her short nightgown barely covers her ass, and her nipples are pebbled against the thin material. No bra. *Shit!* This is pure fucking torture. I really should be nominated for sainthood for being able to keep my hands to myself.

"I've really missed you." She pulls me closer, shocking me by licking the seam of my lips. I suck in a breath as my cock grows painfully hard in my pants.

"What are you doing, baby girl?" I ask, stroking her back, and moving my hands dangerously close to her luscious ass.

"Trying to kiss you," I give her a couple of chaste kisses, doing my best not to give in to my baser instincts.

"I want you," she whispers against my lips as she rubs her breasts against me. *Jesus.* I stare at her in shock because I am so stunned. I really thought this desperate need was one-sided and nothing would ever happen between us. To find out she wants me, too? A man only has so much willpower.

I finally relent and deepen the kiss. *Just this once.* It's everything I've imagined and more. She tastes like strawberries and desire. I give in to my instincts and fist her hair while I take her mouth roughly.

"You don't know what you are asking for, baby girl," I growl against her mouth. I lick down her neck, making her moan.

"Oh, but I do." She climbs me like a tree, and wraps her arms and legs around me, bringing her center flush against my hardness. "Oh, Daddy," she moans. "You feel so good. Your cock is so hard."

"Jesus, baby. I'm always hard around you. Since when do you call me Daddy?" I sit down on the couch, never letting go of her. We continue kissing as she starts grinding against me. I can feel her heat through my pants. "Fuck, baby girl. You're killing me."

She grinds harder. "You feel so good. I want you inside me so badly. Please fuck me, Daddy." she whispers in my ear. I nearly come just hearing her say that. I never knew I had a thing for that, but it just seems right with her. *Shit!* As much as I want her, this is getting out of control really fast. I know that I need to be the one to put a stop to it.

"Sweetheart, you know I can't do that." She pouts at me. "You can rub against me, though, baby. Just this once. Use me to get yourself off." It's wrong. I know it is, but I need her so much; just some little bit of her. Her eyes darken as she grinds against me harder. When she comes, her whole body shakes and I feel her wetness against my leg. It's the sexiest damn thing I've ever seen. I spill in my pants like a fucking teenager.

I hold her close to me and sigh. I can't resist cupping her breasts through her nightgown and pinching her nipples. "You know this can't happen again, sweetheart. You might want me now, but for how long? I'm too old for you, and I'm your guardian."

I sniff her hair, breathing in her delicious scent as I pepper kisses down her neck, making goosebumps break out on her skin. I suck her nipple through her clothes, making her moan. I take my time kissing and squeezing her gorgeous tits through her clothes. *Just this once.*

She looks up at me, licking her lips and pushing her hips toward mine. "You're not too old, and I'm an adult now. I'll always want you, and the whole guardian/ward thing doesn't matter anymore."

I know that it still does, but I don't want to think about it tonight. We kiss and grind for a bit before we settle down for the night. I have everything I need and want in the world in my arms right now. I hold her close as she plasters herself against me. We spend the night sleeping on the couch snuggled against each other.

Ryder

"Well, this is cozy." I hear my mother's voice from far away.

"Mimi!" I hear Nichole squeal. *Oh, shit.* I pry my eyes open and look up at my mom hugging her tightly. I can tell from the disapproving look on her face that we'll be having a long conversation soon.

"It's so good to see you, Nichole. It's been too long. I missed you, dear."

"I missed you, too. I wish you would move back to town," she smiles.

"I know. I may eventually. I'm just a few hours away, though. Sweetheart, why don't you go get ready and the three of us can spend the day together?"

"That sounds great!" she kisses us both on the cheek and bounces off to get ready. I run my fingers through my hair and prepare for the inquisition I'm about to face. The military should hire my mother. She may be all of five-foot-one, but Rachel Richards can put the screws to you like no other. She could topple governments single-handedly without saying a word.

She whacks my head with one of the couch pillows. "What the hell are you playing at, Ryder? Haven't I taught you better than this?"

"Ouch! That hurt," I say, rubbing my head. "What are you talking about?" She looks down her nose at me. I take stock of my appearance. It really doesn't look good. I took my shirt off last night and unbuttoned my pants. I look pretty disheveled and had Nichole sleeping on top of me all night in next to nothing.

"That girl is in love with you-always has been, always will be. You'd better not start anything with her unless you plan on making it permanent. It would break her heart. I love that girl like my own. If you hurt her, I'll kick your ass!"

I laugh at the thought of this tiny woman doing damage to me, though I have no doubt she could make it happen. "She's not in love with me, Mom, but I get it. I can't let anything happen. I know it would be wrong."

"And why is that?"

"Because I'm her guardian."

She sighs. "Sweetheart, she's twenty-two; not sixteen. If she was a minor, I totally agree that it would be extremely inappropriate, not to mention illegal, but she's a grown woman. I think you are making a much bigger deal about this than you need to. Life is short. I know that better than anyone. If you want to be together, be together. Just don't lead her on if all you want is a fling."

I don't just want a fling with Nichole; I want everything. Mom's words give me food for thought, but I know that, regardless, I'm still way too old for Nichole. She could have anyone she wants. Why would she want someone eighteen years her senior? She should have someone closer to her age. Why does the idea of that make me want to murder someone?

We spend the whole day with Mom. She ends up spending the night with us, too. I lock myself in my room to avoid the temptation of Nichole. I have a feeling I may need to do that from now on. Now that I know she feels something for me, too, how much longer will I be able to control myself? If and when my control finally snaps, God help us both.

Nichole

♥

"You're never here," I pout, tossing my magazine down. Ryder has been staying away from me even more than usual after what happened between us last week. He even started locking his bedroom door at night, to keep me out, I assume.

"I've just been busy lately, Nikki."

"Well, it sucks. And you know I hate that nickname!" I yell, acting every bit the child he probably still thinks I am. I take a calming breath. Back to my plan. I hug him, and give him a kiss on the mouth before deepening it.

"Nichole," he groans, before taking my mouth harder. "We can't do this again."

"I don't know why not." I huff as he sets me away from him. After a few moments, I walk to the kitchen. I pretend to look through the cabinets for a snack. "Hmmm. Is there anything good in here? See anything you'd like to eat, Daddy?" I ask, bending over in my short skirt and giving him a clear view of my very naked ass and pussy. What can I say? Subtlety hasn't worked so far, so maybe a more forceful approach will.

He sucks in a breath before he charges toward me like a man on a mission. He picks me up like I weigh nothing, making me squeak loudly, and carries me to the couch. Before I can react, he turns me over his lap, and spanks my naked ass again and again, until my cheeks are probably red from his hand print.

The first couple of smacks cause me to yelp, but after that, I just moan; loudly. I had no idea that being spanked would be such a turn-on. I don't think it would be with anyone else, but with Ryder, it definitely is. Between that and the stiffness I feel growing underneath me, I am about to spontaneously combust. I squirm against him, seeking relief.

"What did I do to deserve a spanking, Daddy?" I bat innocent looking eyes at him.

"You know exactly what you did, baby girl. You were trying to tempt me into throwing you down and fucking you senseless."

I moan, just imagining him thrusting his cock inside me. "Did it work?"

"No, baby. It didn't work. It can't happen. It's wrong. So fucking wrong, no matter how much I might want it." Even as he says this, he slides a finger into my dripping wet cunt. "Fuck, baby. You feel so good. You are already drenched for me. I think that spanking turned you on."

"It did, but I'm always wet for you. Please, Ryder. I need you."

"I can't fuck you, baby, but I can still make you feel good." He pushes two fingers inside me, making me moan as I clench around him. "You like that, don't you?"

"Yes!"

He fucks me faster and faster with his thick fingers, before pinching my clit and sending me spiraling. "That's it, baby. Fuck my fingers like a good girl." I moan again and drench him with my juices. "So fucking sexy," he says, licking his fingers. "And so fucking delicious.

Your cream tastes so good, baby girl. Now I'm going to fill you up with mine."

"Yes! Please!" He jerks his cock out of his pants just in time to shoot his cream inside my needy pussy. I reach out and squeeze it, not even able to wrap my hand around his thickness. I moan and try to push his cum further inside me so his seed will take root. I stroke him more. "I love feeling your hot cum in me. Will you please fuck me now?"

He drops his head back against the couch, and removes my hands from his cock. "We can't, baby girl. It would be so wrong. I'm so sorry, sweetheart. I should never have touched you at all, but I really crossed the line tonight. I just want you so damn much. I lose my fucking mind when I'm around you. You are so damn irresistible. Let's just forget anything ever happened between us."

He gives me a quick kiss on the head and rushes off to his room. Tears stream down my face as I watch him retreat. I have a pity party for myself for several minutes before I dry my eyes and strengthen my resolve. No. He is wrong. Neither one of us is going to be able to forget what just happened. He wants this just as much as I do. If I have anything to say about it, this won't be the end of our story; it will just be the beginning.

The next night, I open the door to the master bathroom and view heaven, or hell, depending on your way of thinking. I close my eyes and open them again, sure I must be dreaming.

Nichole's very naked, voluptuous body is glistening wet from the bath. Her gorgeous, perfect tits, sweet pussy, and tight ass I've dreamed of so many times are on full display for me, with only a few feet separating us. It's the most tempting sight I've ever seen.

I stare for several beats before I realize I need to get the hell out of here; immediately. My mind knows, but my feet are rooted to the floor. And my cock? He's hard as stone. Images of me pounding into her sweet little pussy until she begs me to stop go through my mind on repeat.

I finally look up at her beautiful face to see her smiling seductively at me. "I didn't know you were home yet, Uncle Ryder. I really wanted to try out your giant tub. You don't mind, do you?" I grunt at her. It's all I'm capable of at the moment.

She walks toward me, throwing more temptation in my path than she can possibly understand. She wraps herself in a towel as she kisses me on the mouth and gives me a long hug, pressing every inch of her gorgeous body against mine. I clench my fists and dig my fingernails into my palms to keep from reaching for her. It takes every ounce of my self-control to not rip her towel off and bury my dick in her glistening slit. She smiles over her shoulder at me and heads toward her room, having just rocked my entire world off its foundation.

I throw my clothes off haphazardly, and push my bedroom door shut. I need to get myself under control before I toss Nichole on my bed and keep her there until I've fucked my baby into her.

Nichole

♥

Was that enough to make his control finally snap? Lord, I hope so. I've never been naked in front of anyone before. I'm shaking from nerves and need. Ryder's cock was so hard, it was very obviously straining against his jeans. The temptation to grab it was overwhelming, but I want to make him lose control completely before I do that.

I toss on a see-through nightie and walk back toward his room. The door isn't completely shut, and I hear noises. I inch it open, only to see all my fantasies in the flesh. Ryder is completely naked, and lying on top of his comforter, roughly stroking his huge cock. My arousal drips down my legs as I look on with lust filled eyes. I am not about to let this opportunity go to waste.

I walk toward him, touching his legs as I kneel between them. He stops, looking down at me and moaning. "Nichole, baby, you shouldn't be here," he rasps out.

"Let me help, Daddy. I want to make you feel good," I say, grabbing his angry cock and putting it in my mouth. It's so large, I can only get a few inches in, but I feel him spurting a bit immediately, so I must be doing something right. I lick him like a lollipop, taking as much of him as I can. He tastes even better than I imagined. "Mmmm. Delicious."

"Fuck, baby girl. You can't do this," he protests for a moment, but makes no move to stop me. I massage his balls and stroke him. I suck him even further down my throat, causing me to gag and making my pussy drip with pleasure. Who knew that pleasing him would make me feel so good?

After a minute, he stops protesting and starts encouraging me. "That's so good, sweetheart. Such a good girl. Suck my big cock. Make me come down your throat." I double down on my efforts. He's helping me now, fucking my mouth with his huge member as he controls my head movements with his hand. The sting of his hand pulling my hair increases my pleasure even more. He cries out as he explodes in my mouth. I swallow stream after stream of his salty cum as I feel my own release rocket through my body.

He lies back, catching his breath. I crawl on top of him, kissing his mouth with everything I've got. He caresses me, then squeezes my butt cheeks. "We can't keep doing this, baby girl. It's wrong."

"Why is it so wrong?" I ask, exploring his chest and arms with my wandering hands. I kiss his face and neck, working my way down his chest, and making him moan.

"Because I raised you. I'm your fucking guardian, for Christ's sake. What would people think?"

"I've never known you to care what anyone thinks. Besides, I'm a grown woman now."

"Don't I fucking know it."

I look him in the eye, letting him know how serious I am. "Ryder, we're not related. You're not my father," I say as I kiss him. "But you could be my daddy," I whisper against his ear before nibbling on it. He tenses at my words and his cock is hard as stone once again. "Please, Daddy. I ache for your big cock to fill me up. My pussy feels so empty without it."

"Fuck, baby. You have no idea how much I want that, but I can't. It's so fucking wrong. I have to taste you, though. Just this once, then I'll stop." I readily agree as he moves between my legs and immediately devours my needy pussy. I nearly jump off the bed at the unfamiliar sensation. He holds me down with one arm while he uses his tongue and fingers to torture me with pleasure, driving me over the edge, again and again. He sucks my clit into his mouth, hard, and I nearly black out from the pleasure.

He gathers my boneless body in his arms and holds me close. He feels so warm all over, and his cock is still standing at attention. "You taste so good, baby girl. I could eat your pussy every day." I moan at the image his words evoke. He tosses my nightie across the room and thrusts against me. He squeezes my breasts as he sucks one nipple into his mouth, then the other. His every touch sets me on fire. I need more. I need everything he has to give.

I wrap my fingers around his cock as I lick his ear. "Couldn't we do just a little more? You could just put the tip of your cock inside me? Please? Wouldn't that feel good?" I say, hoping to tempt him into taking me.

He moans, squeezing my breasts harder. "Okay, baby girl. Just the tip, to give us both a little taste, then I'll pull out."

He pushes me down and, true to his word, puts just the tip of his cock inside me. "Damn, baby. This pussy is so tight, but you are already soaking wet for me. I bet you'd take me so good."

"I know I would, Daddy. I'm always so wet for you. More, please."

"I shouldn't, baby," he says, clenching his teeth, but pushing in a little more. His body shakes with restraint. I lift my hips up, forcing him in a few more inches. "Fuck, baby girl. Want to fuck you so bad. You have no idea how hard it is to hold back from doing all the filthy things I want to do to you."

"Then do them. Please, Ryder. I don't want to be your ward; I want to be your woman. No one else has ever had me. I've saved myself for you; only you. Please fuck me. I ache for you. My pussy is so hungry for you. I love you. Please fill me up with your cum and make me yours forever."

"Fuck!" he yells as he slams through my barrier, filling me to the brim with his giant cock.

"Yes!" I scream, overcome with the pleasure of finally being filled by him.

"Fuck, baby. I shouldn't have done that, but I can't stop now. I should go slow, but I can't. I have to fuck your perfect pussy now. I've wanted this for far too long. I can't hold back any longer."

He's out of control now, fucking me into the mattress. His strong thrusts make the bed squeak loudly. I had no idea anything could feel this good. I moan his name repeatedly as he gives me more pleasure than I have ever felt. I feel my juices slide down my legs as he hits my g-spot over and over again, making me come several times with his hard thrusts. "That's it, baby girl. You're taking me so good. Come all over Daddy's big cock."

"Yes!" I scream as I soak him with my juices once more. He lifts me up, impaling me on his cock and fucking me even harder. He's somehow even deeper inside now. My inner walls spasm hard, milking him as he groans, shooting rope after rope of cum into my ripe womb. I really hope he just got me pregnant.

He pulls me against his chest. "I don't think you know what you've gotten yourself into, baby girl," he says as he spreads kisses all up and down my body, making me squirm with need again. "Now that I've had you, I won't be able to let you go; ever. I don't care what the fuck anyone else thinks anymore. If we have to move to the other side of the world, we will. All that matters is that we are together now. I love you, baby. You are mine."

"I love you, too."

"I'm going to fuck your hot little pussy every day. I'm your daddy now. I'll take good care of you, and you are going to be Daddy's good little girl. You'll give me your creamy little cunt whenever and wherever I want."

I moan, loving that idea. "Yes, Daddy. I want that so much."

Ryder

I haven't been to work for a week now. Why? Because I've been too busy fucking Nichole every chance I get. We have spent lots of time together outside of bed, too, but all it takes is a glimpse of her sexy body and I'm on her like a ravenous beast. She's mine now, and I make sure to remind her of that every chance I get.

I've fucked her on the dining table, the kitchen counter, and even the floor. Wherever I take her, she eagerly spreads her legs for me. For some reason, she seems to want me as much as I want her. Thank fuck!

I'm a fiend for her. I've never been so out of control. I pray that I've already put my baby in her. The thought of her round with my child turns me on like nothing else. Is this really wrong? I don't care anymore. All I care about is Nichole. She is mine, now and forever. End of story.

I'm sitting at my home office desk, trying to catch up on emails when she walks in. "What are you doing, Daddy?"

"Just some work, baby. Let me finish up a couple of things." She starts playing on one of my computers while she waits.

"What's this?" I turn to see what she's looking at. *Fuck!* It's my worst nightmare. She has found the file with all the surveillance pictures and videos of her I have on my computer. "Are there cameras all through the house? In my room?" she whispers.

She sounds upset. I drag my hand across my beard, prepared to plead my case to this beautiful girl. I can't lose her. I would go insane. "Yes, sweetheart, there are cameras in the rest of the house, but not in your room or your bathroom."

"Why?" she asks cautiously.

"Because I'm fucking obsessed with you, little girl. I have been for close to a year now. I did everything I could to stay away from you as much as possible. I had to be able to at least see you, though. I feel better if I can at least watch you."

She looks thoughtful for several minutes. "Is there anything else?"

"What do you mean?"

"Is there anything else you've done that I don't know about."

I sigh. I don't want to scare her, but I know if I lie, and she somehow finds out, I will lose her. "Sometimes I go into your room after you go to sleep and watch you." She raises an eyebrow at me. "Sometimes I jack off and spread it across your skin."

"Oh my gosh!" she jumps up, then paces back and forth for several minutes. She finally stops, and looks at me. "Why did you do those things?"

"Because I love you so fucking much! You are all I think about; all I want. Please believe me, baby girl. I know that it's sick and wrong, and I'll do my best to stop."

She contemplates me for a few moments before motioning for me to sit back in my chair. "I know I should be appalled, but it's really kind of sexy. And sweet."

"Sweet?" I ask, too stunned to say much more.

"I realize I should be upset, but it turns me on thinking about you watching me," she says, kissing me gently.

"I'm so glad, baby. I'm sorry I watched you without you knowing."

"Well, I mean, maybe I should apologize, too. I watched you swim naked and jack off without you knowing it."

"What!? You little minx!" I say, swatting her butt.

"Don't stop watching me, Daddy. I like it. In fact, you can put a camera in the bedroom if you like. I hope I'll be in your bed from now on, though," she says, straddling me. She kisses my neck while she rubs against me. She brings my fingers in between her legs to find her dripping naked cunt.

"It turns me on thinking about you doing those things. Why don't you stop working for the day? You might need to remind me who I belong to."

I growl. "You belong to me. Fuck, baby. You know I can't resist you. Work will have to wait."

She smiles. "That's what I'm counting on."

I push down my pants and slam her onto my aching cock.

"Ryder!" she screams.

"Can't stop fucking you, baby. All I want to do, every second of the damn day." I slam her down on me harder and harder. I shred her nightgown and suck her nipple into my mouth, making her come again. "So fucking responsive, baby girl. Daddy has to fuck you harder now."

"Yes, Daddy!" she cries. I lay her on my desk and pound into her pussy with all my might. The civilized man I normally am has been replaced by the beast who wants this woman above all else. I'm beyond obsessed, and, thank God, she's okay with that; even likes it. I don't have to hold anything back anymore.

"You are mine!" I scream, claiming her juicy cunt again and again. "Gonna put my baby in you, sweetheart. You want that, don't you?"

"Yes, Daddy. So much." I pinch her clit as I come inside her, filling her once more. I hold her for several minutes before carrying her back to my bedroom and fucking her so many times, I lose count.

Ryder

As much as I want to stay in my happy bubble with Nichole, we eventually have to go back to real life. My first full day back at work is a bitch. I have a ton of meetings and way too many emails to catch up on.

Even though I have great people working for me at Ryder Industries, there's still a lot for me to take care of. I've built this place up to be one of the top manufacturers of prefab homes in the country. We can barely keep up with the demand these days.

We've had some computer issues recently, so Nikki has spent the day looking through our cybersecurity to see where we are vulnerable. When it comes to that shit, she is fucking brilliant. She's better with computers than anyone I've ever seen.

She comes in, shutting the door behind her. "You've got major problems."

"Seriously?"

"Yes, seriously. A five-year-old could break into your system. Let me show you." She steps over to my desk and shows me all the issues she found. She is right. There are way too many of them.

"How long will it take to fix everything?"

"It won't be quick, or cheap."

I pull her into my lap. "Come work for me, permanently." I say, kissing her neck.

"What?"

"Come work for me. You can be the head of cybersecurity. I want you here with me. I want the best, and you are definitely the best. Plus, I can't handle being away from you for any length of time." I say, kissing her mouth. "High salary, great benefits, and a boss who's completely obsessed with you."

She giggles. "Really, now? What kind of great benefits would I get from this obsessed boss?"

"Let me demonstrate." I lock the door and spend the rest of the day convincing Nichole to come work for me.

Nichole

♥

I wake up slowly, stretching, when something on my finger snags the comforter. *What on earth?* I look down to see a stunning square cut diamond ring on my finger. I close my eyes and reopen them; sure I am dreaming, but the sparkling ring is still there. It is so big, but absolutely gorgeous.

"Did he propose and I missed it?"

"No, sweetheart. He didn't, because it's not a question of if, it's a question of when."

I look over at Ryder and smile widely, thrilled that things are moving so quickly, and we are on the same page. I mean, we have known each other forever, but we've only been together for a couple of weeks. I could understand if he wanted us to date for a while first, but I'm thrilled that's not the plan. "Really? So, when is it you plan on marrying me?"

"As soon as humanly possible, baby girl. I can't live without you. I love you with all my heart."

"I love you, too." I'm so glad he wants us to be together forever, too. I throw my arms around him. One kiss leads to another, until we lose all sense of time. It is well past lunch before we finally start our day.

Ryder

"**C**ome in," I call to the person knocking on my door.

"Sir, may I speak to you for a moment?" Steven Smith, a board member asks.

"Sure thing. How can I help you?"

"There are some rumors going around, sir. The board is concerned about the company's image."

"What rumors?"

"Well, sir, that you are having an inappropriate relationship with the woman who is your very young ward, and now your employee."

I clench my teeth together before I can tell him to go fuck himself. "Steven, she is twenty-two, an adult, and I'm planning to make her my wife as soon as possible."

"Oh. I see." I can see the wheels turning in his head. "Let me talk to the other board members."

He comes back a short time later. "Since she is of age, and you are getting married soon, we could get ahead of the story and put a positive spin on it."

"Sounds great." I grin. One more reason to get the ball rolling. I'm going to marry my baby girl before she has a chance to change her mind. I'm thrilled the board approves, but there was never a choice to be made. If I had to choose between Nichole and the company, I would pick her, hands down, every single time.

Speaking of which, I finally put a call in to Mom. "How quickly can you throw a wedding together?" Her squealing nearly deafens me, but I'm glad to know she is so happy about our upcoming nuptials.

Nichole

♥

Friday night, I come home from running errands to find Ryder packing a bunch of stuff into our suitcases. "Are we going somewhere?"

"Yes, we are, baby girl," he says, giving me a lingering kiss. "You might make sure I didn't forget anything important of yours. We'll be gone for several days. You should probably bring your laptop, just in case."

A short time later, we are in the car driving to our mystery destination. Trying to get information out of him is like pulling teeth. He should have been a spy. No secrets would ever be given up by him.

"Where are we going?"

"I told you, it's a surprise."

I huff loudly. "I don't like surprises."

He smiles. "Yes, you do, baby. Don't lie to Daddy."

I huff again, knowing he speaks the truth. I actually love surprises. "Fine."

We are in the car for so long, I eventually fall asleep. When I wake up, I can't believe my eyes. "Where are we?" I look around at the gorgeous log cabin in front of us.

"This is where we will be staying for a couple of weeks. We still have WiFi, if you need to work some, but I'm hoping we can mostly forget about work while we are here."

"Okay. So, just a relaxing trip, then?"

"No, baby," he pulls me closer. "A honeymoon."

"A honeymoon? How can we have a honeymoon when we haven't even gotten married yet?"

"Baby, there's a beautiful chapel right down the road where we can get married. I know you want Mom there, and a few other people. I've arranged everything."

"But, a dress," I protest.

"Mom brought several in your size for you to try on. Her friend owns a bridal shop, and she was more than happy to help. I thought we could get married tomorrow. What do you say?"

"I say yes!" I screech, hugging him tight. I can't believe at this time tomorrow, I will be Mrs. Ryder Richards. I feel like all my dreams are coming true.

Ryder

The wedding came together beautifully, mainly thanks to Mom. No one can throw a lavish event on short notice like she can. I've never seen so many flowers in my life, but I know Nichole will love them, along with the cupcakes she loves from *Tempting Treats*.

When she and Mom walk down the aisle toward me, I am stunned by Nichole's beauty. She's always gorgeous, but even more so today. She looks like a princess in the glittery white gown that shows off her curves. She absolutely glows. I am the lucking fucking bastard in the world.

She smiles up at me when Mom hands her off to me, sniffling away and swiping at tears. I think she's almost as happy as us that we are getting married. I grab Nichole and kiss her passionately, while I profess my love for her.

After a few minutes, I hear lots of laughs and throat clearing. I look down to see her grinning up at me. "I love you so much, baby girl."

"I love you, too, Daddy. Now, let's get married."

The wedding goes by in the blink of an eye, then we are on to the reception. Thankfully, we only invited a handful of guests, so it's not an overly long event. Before long, my beautiful wife whispers in my ear.

"Hey, husband. Are you planning to fuck your new wife anytime soon?" I smile at her.

"You know it, baby girl. Let's tell everyone goodbye and get the hell out of here."

A short time later, we are back at our cabin. I'm happy we got to share our day with the people we love the most, but, right now, the only person I want to be with is my wife. "I can't believe how lucky I am to have you, baby," I say, holding her against me.

"Don't forget it," she sasses. "How lucky we both are. I love you so much, Ryder."

"I love you, too, baby. Let me show you how much."

In the space of a few minutes, I have her intricate dress off of her, leaving her in gorgeous white lingerie. "Damn, baby. You look so gorgeous."

"Thank you." I enjoy the view as she walks back to me. Her bustier is nipped in at the waist, and pushes her breasts up until they are nearly overflowing the cups. Add to that, the tiny thong, garters, and thigh high stockings, and she is the sexiest fucking thing I have ever seen.

"So sexy, baby. Can't believe you are finally mine."

"Believe it. I'm yours, and you're mine. Take me, Daddy. Please."

I toss her onto the bed, making her giggle. I pop her breasts out of her bustier and suck on them until she squirms, needing more of me. I thrust against her pussy. She's so wet and ready, I can feel it through my slacks. I jump back up and strip in seconds, ready to be inside my beautiful wife.

"So wet. So beautiful. Have to taste you first, baby girl." I quickly toss her thong off her and zero in on her glistening slit. I lick and finger her, bringing her to a peak again and again, until she begs for more.

"Please, Daddy. I need you to fuck me." When I feel precum bubbling from my cock, I thrust inside her, eliciting moans from both of us.

"Fuck, baby. You feel so good. I can't be gentle right now. Daddy needs to fuck you hard."

"Yes, Daddy! Please fuck me as hard as you want. I want you so much." I'm out of control now, slamming into her wet heat harder and harder. The room is silent except for the squelching sound of me pounding inside her hot cunt.

I rip the rest of her lingerie off so that I have access to every inch of her beautiful body. I take turns sucking and nibbling on her nipples, sending her over the edge several times. When I can't hold on any longer, I pinch her clit, sending her into a full body orgasm, as I fill her with my seed.

We are both boneless as we snuggle together. "Happy wedding day, beautiful wife." I kiss her gently.

"Happy wedding day, handsome husband."

As perfect as this day has been, the best part is knowing that we have the rest of our lives together.

Epilogue—Nichole

♥

Six weeks later...

Why am I so tired? It's Saturday, so I can sleep in, but it's ten o clock! I *never* sleep this late. Late for me is more like eight. For some reason, I've been really exhausted lately. Maybe I need to change vitamins.

My handsome husband suddenly appears in the doorway, bringing food. What a prince! "Breakfast in bed for my princess."

"Oh, my gosh! That is so sweet of you," I manage before the scent of bacon hits me, making my stomach roll. I rush to the bathroom, barely making it to the toilet before I throw up everything in my stomach. *Gross.*

"Are you okay, baby girl?"

I nod as I brush my teeth and gargle with mouthwash to get the disgusting taste out of my mouth. "I think so. I'm so sorry, Ryder. I know you went to a lot of trouble, but can you please take the bacon away? The smell is really bothering me, for some reason."

"Sure, sweetheart." He comes back in a few minutes and leans against the wall, studying me like a science experiment.

"You are acting really weird. Why are you watching me?"

He grins. "I always watch you, baby girl. You know that. I'm watching you right now because I'm pretty sure you are carrying my child."

"What? Why on earth would you say that?" My voice trails off as I think about all of my symptoms. I'm exhausted, I'm bothered by smells, I just threw up, and my boobs seem to be getting bigger. Now that I think about it, I can't remember the last time I had a period. "Oh my gosh! I guess I should take a test."

"No problem, sweetheart." He reaches inside the vanity and pulls out a pink box, smiling at me.

"When did you buy this?"

"As soon as we got together," he grins. "Power of positive thinking and all that. Take it and we can know for sure."

A few minutes later, we stare at the plus sign on the little stick. Ryder is grinning from ear to ear. "Congratulations, Mommy."

I smile back at him. "Congratulations, Daddy. You managed to knock me up in record time." I hug him tight.

"That I did, baby girl. That I did. Now I'll have you and a baby made from our love."

"That's so sweet," I get out before tears well in my eyes. Hormones. *Ugh.*

"I love you so much, baby girl."

"I love you, too, Daddy."

THE END

If you enjoyed this steamy collection, please take a moment to leave a review. It really helps newer authors like myself. Thank you!

Love,

Lacy

https://lacy-jane.mailchimpsites.comSign up on my website to read a bonus epilogue and see what Ryder and Nichole are up to.

About the Author

L acy Jane is a happily married empty nester and dog mom who believes in happily ever afters and loves to write about them. She enjoys reading steamy romances, streaming shows, and watching football and baseball. She loves hanging out with her husband, kids, friends, family, and dogs. She enjoys traveling, shopping, drinking delicious coffee drinks, and is a self-professed beauty junkie who spends way too much time and money in Sephora and Ulta. Her books are always OTT, high heat, instalove, no cheating, and (of course!) have an HEA. Always a steamy read with HEA guaranteed!

Sign up on my website to be notified of new releases and get freebies from time to time!

https://lacy-jane.mailchimpsites.com

Amazon Author Page

http://www.amazon.com/author/lacyjane

Facebook

https://www.facebook.com/author.lacy.jane

Lacy Jane

Also by Lacy Jane

♥

The Obsessed Alphas Collection

Books 1-4

https://www.amazon.com/dp/B0DDVNW494

This very steamy series has everything you want in a hot, steamy short-always a strong heroine who knows what she wants, and a sexy alpha man who will do anything to get and keep the woman he is obsessed with. This series can be read in any order as each book is a stand alone with no cliffhanger. Each book is OTT with high heat, instalove, no cheating, and (of course!) a HEA. Always a steamy read with HEA guaranteed! Enjoy!

Includes:
Seduced by the Witness
Seducing My Wife
Seducing Her Stalker
Seducing Shelly

Forbidden

Attractions Series

Scorching hot, forbidden relationships!

https://www.amazon.com/dp/B0D487TV3J

These couples shouldn't be together because it's forbidden, but they just can't help themselves. Each is an extra-steamy, OTT, instalove, with extremely high heat, no cheating, and (of course!) a HEA. Always a steamy read with HEA guaranteed!

The Tempting Treats Collection
https://www.amazon.com/dp/B0D6LFKPKJ

Cute, extra-steamy, OTT, instalove short stories, set in a small town.

The Abbott triplets move to Cedar Falls, Montana to open their bakery, Tempting Treats. Little do they know that they are each about to meet the man of their dreams. Meet Aurora,

Avery, and Audrey and enjoy their hot, whirlwind romances! This series is sweet, steamy, and OTT with high heat, instalove, no cheating, and (of course!) a HEA. Always a steamy read with HEA guaranteed! Enjoy!

Sweets for the Sheriff

The first book in my new Tempting Treats series!

Aurora Abbott is the most tempting treat Sheriff Garrison James has ever seen. He is instantly smitten with the sexy little baker, and is determined to make her his. The chemistry between them is undeniable, and it's not long before passion ignites.□

As their whirlwind romance heats up, Aurora finds herself falling hard for the sexy sheriff, but is overcome with fear and uncertainty. Can Garrison push past her walls and make her his, permanently?

Hudson's Sweet Honey

Can a steamy night with a stranger turn into happily ever after? Find out in this racy, instalove romance.

When Hudson meets Avery, he instantly knows she is the one, but she assumes he doesn't want anything serious. After an unforgettable night of passion, he knows he will never let her go. She is his. He just needs to convince his little goddess that he's all in. How will he accomplish that? By putting a baby in her belly and a ring on her finger.

Cupcakes for Colton

When Audrey takes a stray dog to the vet, she comes face to face with a seriously hot veterinarian and his package that she can't take her eyes off of. After a funny, steamy, meet cute, Colton vows to do whatever it takes to make this awkward, adorable woman his for life.

This very adult fairy tale is hot, hot, hot! If you prefer your romances sweet and squeaky clean, this is not the book for you. On the other hand, if you like racy, steamy romances with sexy heroes and strong heroines, this is right up your alley.

This is the second book in my series Once Upon a Time: Twisted Sexy Fairy Tales. Each book is a stand alone, though characters from the other stories occasionally make appearances. As always, this book has high heat, no cheating, instalove, and (of course!) a HEA.

My books are for those who like their happily ever after a little on the dirty side. Always a steamy read with HEA guaranteed. Enjoy!

Enticing Ella (A Billionaire, Older Man, Younger Woman, Steamy Short): Once Upon a Time: Twisted Sexy Fairy Tales Book 3

After a night of passion with Prince, Ella disappears. Now that he has claimed her, Prince will stop at nothing to find Ella and make her his bride. Can he save her from her evil stepmother in time? Find out in this sweet, spicy, modern version of Cinderella, complete with a ball, one evil stepmother, a fairy godmother of sorts, and Ella's adorable little dog, Cujo.

As with all of my books, this contains high heat, instalove, no cheating, and (of course!) a HEA. My books are always a steamy read with HEA guaranteed! Enjoy!